Praise for the Works of Dave Duncan

"Dave Duncan has long been one of the great unsung figures of Canadian fantasy and science fiction, graced with a fertile imagination, a prolific output, and keen writerly skills. With this new novel, Duncan again forges a bold new world, populated with varied and complex characters, distinctive cultures, and a complex system of mythology and science."
— *Quill & Quire*

"That supreme trickster Dave Duncan … is an expert at producing page-turning adventure, and Future Indefinite fully lives up to the suspense promised in its title. It's all throughly entertaining, while it leaves us wondering, right down to the final pages, whether the end will fall into the classical category of comedy or tragedy. Quite a performance, Mr. Duncan!"
— *Locus*

"Duncan writes with unusual flair, drawing upon folklore, myth, and his gift for creating ingenious plots."
— *Year's Best Fantasy and Horror*

"Dave Duncan writes rollicking adventure novels filled with subtle characterization and made bitter-sweet by an underlying darkness. Without striving for grand effects or momentous meetings between genres, he has produced one excellent book after another."
— *Locus*

Books By Dave Duncan

The Dodec Books
Mother of Lies
Children of Chaos

The Alchemist
The Alchemist's Apprentice
The Alchemist's Code
The Alchemist's Pursuit

Tales of the King's Blades
The Gilded Chain
Lord of Fire Lands
Sky of Swords
The Monster War

Chronicles of the King's Blades
Paragon Lost
Impossible Odds
The Jaguar Knights

A Man of His Word
Magic Casement
Faerie Land Forlorn
Perilous Seas
Emperor and Clown

A Handful of Men
The Cutting Edge
Upland Outlaws
The Stricken Field
The Living God

The Great Game
Past Imperative
Present Tense
Future Indefinite

The Omar Books
The Reaver Road
The Hunters' Haunt

The Seventh Sword
The Reluctant Swordsman
The Coming of Wisdom
The Destiny of the Sword
The Death of Nnanji

The Brothers Magnus Novels
Speak to the Devil
When the Saints

Stand-Alone Novels
West of January
The Cursed
A Rose-Red City
Shadow
Strings
Hero!
Ill Met in the Arena
Pock's World

Writing as "Sarah B. Franklin"
Daughter of Troy

Writing as "Ken Hood"
Demon Sword
Demon Rider
Demon Knight

WILDCATTER

a novel

Dave Duncan

EDGE SCIENCE FICTION AND FANTASY PUBLISHING
AN IMPRINT OF HADES PUBLICATIONS, INC.

CALGARY

Wildcatter
Copyright © 2012 by Dave Duncan

This is a work of fiction. Names, characters, places, and
incidents are the products of the author's imagination or
are used fictitiously and are not to be construed as real.
Any resemblance to actual events, locales, organizations,
or persons, living or dead, is entirely coincidental.

Edge Science Fiction and Fantasy Publishing
An Imprint of Hades Publications Inc.
P.O. Box 1714, Calgary, Alberta, T2P 2L7, Canada

Edited by Michelle Heumann
Interior design by Janice Blaine
Cover Illustration by Ralph Kermunski

ISBN: 978-1-894063-90-6

EDGE Science Fiction and Fantasy Publishing and Hades Publications, Inc.
acknowledges the ongoing support of the Canada Council for the Arts and the
Alberta Foundation for the Arts for our publishing programme.

Alberta Foundation for the Arts   Canada Council for the Arts   Conseil des Arts du Canada

Library and Archives Canada Cataloguing in Publication
Duncan, Dave, 1933-
    Wildcatter / Dave Duncan. -- 1st ed.
ISBN 978-1-894063-90-6
    I. Title.

PS8557.U5373W54 2012   C813'.54   C2012-902391-4

FIRST EDITION
(E20120507)
Printed in Canada
www.edgewebsite.com

AUTHOR'S NOTE

I was a wildcatter once. To say that this book is based on my own experience would be obvious rubbish. Nevertheless, many years ago, I worked for a succession of small "independent" oil companies, which explored for petroleum, competing against "majors," meaning multinationals with vastly greater resources. Strangely, the Goliaths did not always win. There was a lot of luck in wildcatting, which originally meant hunting for oil and gas "out among the wildcats", far from any known fields.

I had some modest success, and the money I made then helped support me when I left geology for a writing career. I met a lot of fascinating characters. I saw some of the bare-knuckle gold-rush-style towns that grew up near any important discovery.

The tie-in to this story is that people do not change. If interstellar travel ever develops along the lines I suggest, then it will surely attract the same sort of gamblers. If there are riches to be found among the stars, then wildcatters will be out there.

DAY 401

We ignored the protesters shouting slogans outside the gates. Back in those days a lot of kooky people were convinced that every star traveler was going to bring back some weird virus that would wipe out life as we know it. Well, that was fifty years ago and it hasn't happened yet.

Gregor Fonatelles: *My Life in the Big Nothing*
Gogbok 2364.EN.56789

⊷╾◉ ✴ ◉╼⊶

"All hands on deck! All hands on deck!"

That urgent call failed to disturb the syncopated rhythm of two persons breathing in a darkened cabin.

"We've been screwed, dammit!"

Certainly somebody had been. Seth was heavily entangled in soft, smooth arms and legs, two of each, in a soft, warm bed. Whoever it was smelled nice, was alive, gently breathing. Do it again soon, not yet… He sank back into sweet nirvana.

"Captain, hear this!"

"Captain here," Jordan muttered in Seth's ear, her voice still thick with sleep.

"Jordan, there's a freaking flag on the planet!"

That was the voice of First Officer Hanna Finn, who had the watch. Who was so virginally prim that she never, ever used words like "dammit" or "screwed." Was unheard-of. Seth forced open one eye: the wall display showed *401:01:14*.

Made sense.

On *Day 400* there had been a party, which explained why someone was kicking his head with hob nail boots. A fantastic, riotous, bacchanalian celebration of triumph, victory, sugarplum riches in sight at last. All the work and tedium, tension and danger had been forgotten as the Holy Grail of success shone there in the darkness. ISLA's General Regulations prohibited alcohol aboard starships, a law impossible to enforce when synthesizers could convert plant and animal waste into gourmet food. So the party had been memorable, but when it began to grow quirky, Seth had scooped the captain up and carried her off over his shoulder to the cabin they currently shared.

That same Jordan was now making protesting noises and punching him in the ribs. Seemed he had been sleeping more *on top of* than *with*. He parted stickily from her and rolled off. From what he remembered, it had been a rollick to die for, which is what his headache now made seem both likely and devoutly to be wished.

"I'm coming." Jordan threw aside the cover; lights came on; she grabbed her clothes from the chair.

They couldn't have slept more than thirty minutes and Seth was due to relieve Hanna in less than an hour. Whatever could be exciting First so? He slid hairy legs over the edge of the bed and reached down for the shorts and top he had dropped while in too much of a lusting frenzy to think tidy. He went reeling at Jordan's heels as she sped along the corridor into the control room.

The control room was the second largest space in *Golden Hind's* living quarters but fourteen months ago he had considered it poky. His appreciation of size had changed since then. Its walls, ceiling, and even padded floor, could be made to display the surrounding starscape of the galaxy, or scenes such as a boat trip along the Amazon or the hubbub of a Chinese dancing team at a country fair. They were mercifully blank beige now. Hanna sat alone in her place at the long table. Jordan slid into hers at the head, and Seth hurried around to his, at the far end.

Woe betide anyone who dared sit in the wrong chair. As Commodore JC Lecanard never tired of pointing out, rank was important when six people were confined for a long time in cramped quarters; it produced a necessary minimum of formality and respect, he said. Top dogs thought like that. Seth was bottom dog, even if he was the captain's current bed partner He called her "ma'am" when they had their clothes on and rarely needed to talk at all when they didn't.

Hanna looked as if her headache was even more fatal than his. Her long auburnhair, normally a glory, was now a tangled fishing net, her emerald eyes floated in seas of blood. Poor Hanna was so repressed that this might well be her first-ever hangover. Prudish or not, she had proved to be a superb navigator and first officer.

She said, "Look at that awful thing." She meant a 3-D projection of the local Cacafuego planetary system that was currently floating above the table.

The hologram was not to scale, but it showed the central G-type star with one close-in hot gas giant planet whirling around it every three days. Far out the two ice giants marched in eccentric, retrograde orbits. It was this unusual combination that had confounded the Doppler trace of the planets' gravitational action on the star, the main reason that Cacafuego had escaped detection for so long. Cacafuego itself, the world of their dreams, was a shining blue gem right where it ought to be, in the habitable suburbs, neither too hot nor too cold. *With* a single small moon, as they had discovered yesterday. Veteran wildcatters insisted that planets with a single moon were lucky.

But the Cacafuego icon was disfigured now by a glowing, flashing halo that indicated someone had put a radio beacon in orbit around it. That somebody must be presumed human, because a hundred years of stellar exploration had turned up no other species with a knack for technology.

Jordan sighed, did not comment. She was fair, fine-boned, and short of stature. Like most herms, she wore her hair short, but it was still rumpled from sleep and vigorous bed-romping. Her ludicrously smudged eye makeup made her look like a drunken panda.

In stalked JC himself, tucking top into shorts. JC was a huge man, wide, tall, and hairy. At sixty-two, he was easily the oldest person aboard, the originator, sponsor, organizer and leader of the expedition. He slumped into his place on the captain's right, opposite Hanna, and scowled horribly at the holographic display.

"That wasn't there an hour ago. Did they detect us and turn it on?"

—No, Commodore, Control said. —*Two-way response time would be too great at this distance. We have just come within range, and even now the signal is only detectable because we know where to look and can apply sophisticated filtering.*

Astrobiologist Reese Platte entered and took his seat between Seth and Hanna. He glanced around the company with a sneer, which was his usual expression, aided by an overlong nose and chin, a face of bone and angles. Either he had drunk less than the others at the party, or he just found other people's hangovers amusing. Reese was independently wealthy back home and so had less to lose than anyone else.

Lastly came a sleepy Maria Chang, the planetologist, who had obviously taken a moment to brush out her hair. Even sleep deprivation and a hangover could not rob Maria of her poise or seductive walk; her gaze was still sultry as she assessed the others. Maria had no lack of interest in the mission, but she was a people-first person. She took her seat on Seth's right, and then all twelve eyes were directed at the display.

This was *Golden Hind*'s full complement, each of the six having specific skills and duties. Off-duty all that mattered was that they were two men, two women, and two herms. That allowed a lot of different combinations.

Seth waited for someone else to say something. The silence was the sound of crumbling dreams. They had spent fourteen months bottled up in this starship, fourteen months cut out of their lives, with the return trip still to come. Wildcatting was the most dangerous of all legal occupations other than military combat, but it could be the most lucrative. Even Seth, the lowly gofer, could hope to become wealthy on his tiny share in the *Hind*'s voyage.

Back on *Day 0*, when *Golden Hind* left Earth orbit, Hanna had estimated 425 days out. She had beaten her estimate by twenty-five days. Yesterday she had plotted the last jump, promising it would take them right to the destination system. The crew had been gathered in the control room, tense with excitement. She had reported, "Ready to jump, ma'am."

Jordan had laid both hands on the table and ordered the jump.

Everyone had checked the star fields around them. Those had barely changed, but above the consol appeared the holograph with Cacafuego shining blue, the color of water and oxygen and life. No further jumps required — four days' coasting and they would be there. Even JC, ever cagey with praise, had complemented Hanna on an incredible feat of navigation. In minutes Control had reported that close scanning of the system showed no significant variation from predictions, and that neither ship or crew had suffered damage. JC had opened his secret hoard of champagne, and the ship had erupted in frenetic celebration.

That had been last night. This morning Seth was not the only one with a pounding headache, which was a bad condition for dealing with disaster.

He jumped as needle claws dug into his thighs, but it was merely Ship's Cat Whittington seeking a friendly lap. She turned around and settled down, tucking her tail in carefully. A happy soul was Whittington, unconcerned by the total absence of mice within 1500 light years. Seth stroked her and she rumbled, flattering the Big One who fed her, ignoring the other Big Ones' confrontation.

"Time slip!" Reese growled. "Welcome to the twenty-fifth century."

Time slip was always a danger. It could not be predicted. People had returned decades after they had been given up for dead, finding the world they knew changed beyond recognition and their friends aged. Had *Golden Hind* lost a century or so on the way here?

"Flaming shit," JC said at last. "We don't need that. Control, who staked that planet?"

—*No planet in this system is presently staked, Commodore.*

"Then who planted the flag?"

—*Beacon's originator's key is registered to DSS De Soto, exploration vessel owned by Galactic Inc., a company incorporated under the laws of...*

Of course it would be Galactic. Galactic was the billion-ton gorilla of the stellar exploration business. Galactic ships had brought back scores of fantastic chemicals that could be synthesized into pharmaceuticals, supplying all humankind with herm drugs, cancer drugs, Methuselah drugs, and hundreds more. Galactic was Goliath, bigger and more successful than the next three exploration companies combined, thousands of times the size of a startup independent like Mighty Mite Ltd.

"*De Soto* was still in dock orbit when we shipped out," Jordan said. "So the time slip may not be very great."

"It could be a hundred years," Reese countered. "Those beacons are built to last." He enjoyed being devil's advocate.

"We don't know there's been any time slip at all," JC said. "We told Hanna we'd rather get home alive than be rich and dead. Galactic has better hazard maps than it ever releases, no matter what ISLA regulations say. It's notorious for putting its crews at risk by cutting corners."

If the planet had not been staked, what did the beacon mean? Seth was always careful not to trample on the experts' toes. Either they all knew the answer already, or he was the only one who had noticed. Possibly they were all afraid to ask a stupid question. The gofer had no status to lose

"I thought staking flags were green," Seth said. "Control, what does yellow stand for?"

—*Yellow beacon indicates danger, will be recommended for proscription.*

Nobody looked in his direction. The death rate among wild-catters was notorious, but most casualties were among the prospectors, the heroic few who actually set foot on exoplanets. If even Galactic thought a planet was too dangerous to visit, then it must be boiling radioactive snake venom.

Galactic sent out entire fleets, not solo vessels like *Hind*. Galactic included dozens of specialists in its expeditions. A tiny start-up company like Mighty Mite had to crew a ship with jacks-of-all-trades, people with multiple skills. *Golden Hind* carried only one prospector, Seth Broderick, who was also porter, janitor, and general gofer.

"I never heard of quarantine, or proscription," he said.

"Quarantine's from ancient marine law," JC said. "When a sailing ship had plague or yellow fever aboard, it had to fly a yellow flag. In the early days of space travel, everyone feared that life-bearing worlds would harbor bugs or viruses that would be brought back to infect the Earth. So far as I know... Reese, has any wildcatter ever been infected by a local disease on an exoplanet?"

"Very rarely," the biologist said. "It has happened, but exo-planet bacteria and viruses are usually so alien that you would be more likely to catch Dutch elm disease from a lobster. You are in less danger from the infection than from your own immune system over-reacting, but we can control that."

JC grunted agreement. "Control, confirm that Cacafuego is virgin territory."

—*ISLA had no record of any previous exploration, Commodore.*

Which meant only that the ship's files had not been updated since first jump, and so were fourteen months out of date. The evidence showed that someone had beaten them to it.

Seth would kill for a cup of coffee and a long glass of orange juice. Sitting with his back to the mess doorway, he was in the path of all the stale scents of last night's party treats wafting by: wine, chili, ripe cheese, onions, and a few recreational materials not listed on the official manifests. It was his job to tidy up. He should fetch and serve refreshments for the others. To hell with duty, this meeting was too critical to miss.

Jordan was drumming fingernails on the table. "Is there a posting date on the beacon?" she asked.

—*Beacon is still too distant for us to query, Captain.*

"Any ships in orbit there now?" asked JC.

—*No transmissions being detected, Commodore. Target is too distant for visual detection.*

Jordan said, "If they're still there, they must have seen our jump flash when we arrived."

"Not necessarily," JC said. "Control, there must be a text message included."

—*Still too distant even for that. We are presently receiving only the wideband alarm signal, barely distinguishable from galactic background noise.*

"If we left ahead of *De Soto*," asked Reese, the biologist, "how far ahead of us could they have gotten here? I mean, how long, in time? Without allowing for any time slip?" Somehow his questions always sounded like sneers.

"A physicist would say that there was no answer to that question," Hanna snapped, her temper glinting again. She must be blaming herself for this catastrophe; she had lost the race. "When you jump, you twist both space and time, so the uncertainty principle cuts in. We took fifteen jumps. If *De Soto* has better maps of the safe havens, as JC says, they may have relied on those without confirming the jumps were still safe. In theory you could travel the whole distance in no time at all."

"And get your gonads fried by radiation somewhere," JC said. "Or ram a brown dwarf star. Better safe than sorry."

The Big Nothing was not truly empty. It hid radiation belts, dust clouds, gas clouds, solitary comets or planets, and even black holes. They all shifted unpredictably in space-time. Running into any of them at supra-light-speed was normally fatal.

Reese made a snorting noise, an annoying habit of his when male. "Never mind theory. How long in practice?"

"As much as two or three months, maybe," Hanna admitted.

The mood of gloom deepened. Four hundred days ago they had greeted the data on Cacafuego with wild rejoicing. Remote sensing by the trans-Neptunian observatories had indicated a highly promising candidate for a life-bearing world, a mere 1,500 light years away, but there were limits to what remote sensing could detect and many things that could make a planet hostile to humans. Now *De Soto* had made a close appraisal and been scared off by what it saw, or what had happened to its prospectors.

Reese curled his lip. "Finders keepers; first come, first served. Even if we discovered something they missed, could they just take it from us?"

Seth thought not. The rules for staking were very specific. There were no Wild West shootouts in the Big Nothing. Battles were fought back home in the courts, where Galactic could outgun Mighty Mite by a million lawyers to one. Returning explorers had to hand over their ships' memory banks to ISLA, and *Golden Hind*'s now recorded the detection of Galactic's beacon. There must be penalties for ignoring a quarantine.

"Not so," JC murmured, speaking unusually softly for him. "It's who plants a flag first that matters. *De Soto* didn't want it. If we stake it now, it would still be ours."

It would not be his job to plant the flag.

"Danger I do not understand," said Maria, the planetologist. "What danger? Poisonous atmospheres, yes. Lots of worlds have that and are still profitable. Monsters, rarely, and nothing worse than tigers."

She noticed Seth's eyebrows rising and smiled an apology. "Nothing you can't shoot or keep out with an EVA suit, I mean. No little green men or long blue women. Diseases, yes; bacteria, viruses, fungi, all sorts of nasty things have tried to infect us, but none of them could penetrate an EVA suit or withstand our medicines. In a hundred years! So what can be more danger-ous about Cacafuego than risks already met and dealt with on explored worlds?"

No one offered a suggestion.

Jordan said, "We have two choices. We can go on in the hope of finding something that Galactic missed. They may have done us a favor, saved us from blundering into disaster. Or we can set course for the backup target." She looked to JC.

Who growled. "Not so fast, Captain! Control, how many planets have ever been proscribed?"

—*Either six or seven, Commodore, all in the very early days, when records were not so well kept. None in the last seventy years.*

"Seven! How many planets have been explored, even briefly?"

—*Recorded 7,364, but numerous others never registered.*

JC leaned back and wrapped his ugly face in his fearsome but unconvincing grin. He looked triumphantly around the table. "They're bluffing! The odds are only one in a thousand that Galactic really has found a killer world. What better way to chase others away than to post a yellow flag? They can change it to green as soon as they decide the rewards are worth the staking fee. They're probably down there now, working away like busy beavers. Maybe they do this all the time, but nobody has chanced along to catch them at it."

Now he wasn't talking of braving a killer world, he was talking of challenging Galactic as well, and perhaps even ISLA.

Jordan opened her mouth and then closed it without speaking. She seemed absurdly outmatched in a shouting match with JC. He was almost forty years older and at least fifty kilos heavier. Seth suspected he had chosen her for the job precisely because she was unassertive and avoided confrontations. That did not mean she would let herself be bullied into a wrong decision, though.

Jason Christopher Lecanard had first gone into the Big Nothing at twenty-four, the same age Seth was now, on a Bonanza expedition — Bonanza being a major company, one of Galactic's rivals — but he'd signed on as an IT engineer, nothing risky like prospector. Back then even large companies had rewarded crews with royalty interests, and that expedition had struck it rich by staking Nirvana, in the Aquila Sector. Nirvana biology had poured out a torrent of novel antivirals and antibiotics over the next ten years. While JC's share had no doubt been a minute percentage, the payoff had been huge. He'd invested his wealth in other ventures, eventually buying into a middle-sized exploration company, and there his luck had held again, with the discovery of the algal textile that had later been synthesized and sold as starsilk.

Two years ago he had founded Mighty Mite Ltd. and started rounding up investors to help him go wildcatting for himself. Those tightwad money-men would have insisted he put both his own life and fortune on the line too. A billion dollars barely showed in the cost of a starship, and the belief among the crew was that JC was betting the farm, risking every cent he had, on *Golden Hind* and Cacafuego. If it failed, he would be as penniless as Seth.

"Does a yellow flag have legal status as a prohibition?" he growled. He was asking Control, while looking thoughtfully at Seth.

—*No, Commodore. But it is a serious caution.*

Hanna said, "Control, what will ISLA say if we ignore the beacon?" There spoke red hair and Irish ancestry. Hanna stood up to JC better than the captain did.

Computers would not speculate. —*It would largely depend on the results, First. If the Authority judges that you put lives at risk, then you and the captain might lose your licenses, and face other penalties.*

JC didn't like that. He regarded laws as war games for lawyers. "We don't know if they're still there. Even if they are, they don't need to know about us." He laid a hairy hand on the table. "Control, turn off all external transmissions, acknowledge no signals until further notice."

—*Orders in violation of ISLA regulations require confirmation by a licensed officer.*

"Flaming shit!" JC muttered, almost but not quite under his breath.

"I'm not convinced we need to go that far," Jordan said.

"Me neither," said Hanna, more forcefully.

So here it came, seconds out of the ring, the sponsor versus the executive officers. Seth was careful to keep a poker face as he waited to see what happened next. Reese and Maria were doing the same, and the room was silent as vacuum.

Without question, Jordan commanded the ship. If she refused to knuckle under to JC's bullying, he would be powerless to over-rule her. Control and the rest of the crew would back her up. On the other hand, JC represented the owners, and was expedition leader. When they got home he could destroy Jordan's career, probably ruin her with a civil suit. But now he leaned back and smiled with feline confidence, veteran of a million boardroom battles.

He wheedled. "What have we got to lose? They may be long gone. Even if they aren't, provided we go in under radio silence, there isn't a chance in a million they'll notice us, and even if they do, how can they identify us? Even visually — you know interstellar gas will have stripped all the paint off our hull. We'll take a closer look at this planet they want to steal, and if it seems like a winner, we'll send the shuttle down, and young Seth there can plant the flag and claim a world for honor and justice. How does that sound, Prospector?" He peered at Seth around the Cacafuego icon.

Only Control ever addressed Seth by his rank. Usually the crew called him gofer, which was supposed to be funny, or cabin boy, which wasn't.

"I'll obey orders, Commodore." The bottom beaver on any totem pole must always kept his head down and never talk back, but he meant orders from the captain and JC knew that.

"There you are, Captain," JC said, all reasonable-like. "Even our hunky hero is in favor."

Jordan said, "Reese, once we go into orbit, how long will it take you to come up with a preliminary appraisal of Cacafuego's potential?"

Reese closed his eyes to activate eyelid implants. His lips and throat moved as he sub-vocalized. "Need to know our trajectory."

While Jordan was telling Control to plot an approach that would minimize the chances of being detected by the Galactic fleet, Seth went back to studying the display. That small moon that JC had named Turd… Most natural satellites orbited above their primaries' equators. There were exceptions; some even moved in retrograde orbits, and Luna was offset as much as twenty-eight degrees. Yesterday Turd had been almost lined up with Cacafuego, and now it was well above, so it must move in a polar orbit, or else… The only satellites that wandered so far from the ecliptic, so far as he knew, were those of the solar planet Uranus, and Uranus itself was tipped over about ninety degrees. Cacafuego might be a very odd world. As planetologist, Maria ought to have noticed that. It wasn't his job to point it out to her.

Even if Cacafuego was severely tilted, why should that make it any more dangerous? Humans needed a twenty-four hour day to satisfy their circadian rhythm, but darkness could be supplied, just as air and temperature could be supplied.

"Very well," Jordan said, offering a compromise. "We can certainly spare four days to enter orbit and four or five days to assess the planet. On *Day 409* or so we'll decide whether to stay or set course for Armada. Control, observe radio silence. All plans subject to change due to circumstance. Acceptable, Commodore?"

"Acceptable, Captain." JC rose up on his hind legs. If a grizzly bear could grin, it might look like that. "Hanna, love, it certainly wasn't your fault that those rascals got here first. Come along, you deserve some sleep." Without waiting for her, he headed out the door.

For a moment Hanna's lips and fists clenched. She was currently JC's roommate, so he had been dropping the sort of hint she detested. Seth's early efforts to woo her had met with no success at all, and he doubted very much that the commodore's had. When the party had started to turn kinky last night, Hanna had been the first to leave, just before Seth had draped the captain over his shoulder and carried her off to the cabin to pursue their fun in private. Whatever the other three had indulged in after that was their business.

She rose and started to walk out, then hesitated. She was still on watch and ISLA rules required that one human be awake at all times. Visibly blushing now, she glanced uneasily at Jordan and then Seth, who nodded agreement and laid a hand on the table.

"Prospector taking the con," he said. That expression always amused him, because it meant steering a ship and no human could steer a starship.

Hanna said, "First Officer going off duty."

—*Confirming Prospector Broderick on watch.*

Hanna left. Even the backs of her ears were red. Reese held out a hand to Maria.

Now Seth could head into the mess to clean up the, um, mess.

Jordan said, "Wait, please, all of you."

The captain came around the table. Seth deposited Whittington on the carpet and rose to accept her outstretched hands. She had trouble meeting his eye.

"He's a lout," she said. "And a bully. But in his way he's also a great man. Nobody knows the Big Nothing better than JC, from the boardroom, all the way down to years of utter boredom. He's made more money in his career than any of us can dream of; he's risking every cent of it. He put this thing together, Seth. Without him none of us would be here. We certainly can't deny him a look at his world. *But* I am not going to let him send you downside to fry in some sort of planetary hell, no matter what he says. Understand?"

Yes, Seth understood, perhaps better than she did, because he knew exactly how JC could make the prospector dance to his tune.

"I don't go down there unless I want to," he said. "*GenRegs 003.01*, remember? I can refuse any order I consider too dangerous unless you and First agree that my refusal will imperil the ship, and if JC Lecanard tries to get nasty, I'll knock his face off."

Jordan smiled wistfully. "I'd almost like to see that, but it's my problem, not yours. I'm the one who has to put him in his place, and I can't do it as well like this. I'll have to shift, love. You do understand?"

He understood that it felt like a kick in the crotch. Millions of years of evolution said his mate was deserting him. That was his stupid lower brain speaking. They'd only been paired two weeks this time. He had no claim on her, and a herm could never be a mate in the way a real woman could. Jordan was great recreation, nothing more.

"You're being sexist," he said. "Stereotypical. There's no reason why a woman can't put him in his place. Verbally, I mean. If you're planning to punch him on the nose, then I advise against it, no matter which gender you happen to be. Let me do it for you."

She barely smiled. "Not sexist, love. It's just, well I know me, both me's, and I know I can handle JC a lot better when I have visible balls. This is too important to risk a screw-up."

"I understand," he said, struggling to hide his bitterness. "The mission must come first."

"I'll make it up to you later, I promise, on the way home."

"It can't be better than it has been, but I'll take the rain check."

He turned to the others, who were watching. Ever since the ship left Earth, the herms had tried to maintain the balance among the crew, never being the same gender at the same time. "Maria, take her over and make her over."

"You're a brute, Seth Broderick." Maria shot him a wink as she came to rescue Jordan. Any other time a wink from Maria would raise his heartbeat twenty points.

Maria and Jordan left together. Two blue pills a day and a high protein diet would make Jordan male again in about three days. But the change would be much easier for them if they shared a cabin with a woman during that time — inhaling female phero-mones, although it was indelicate to mention that. The captain might be right in thinking she would resist JC's bullying better as a man, but it would be because JC wouldn't push a man as hard. Bullying women was an ancient custom, much safer than bullying other men.

Reese came wandering along the room, wearing their usual sardonic half-smile. They were tall for a herm, taller than Seth, although they had a dancer's athletic slimness, nothing like his fighter bulk. Also like him, they had thick hair, wavy and jet black; Seth fought a constant battle against beard shadow, but herms rarely grew facial hair. Reese's only razor was a sense of humor that sounded aggressive when they were male and snide when female.

"So you've been kicked out of the captain's cabin," he said, standing closer to Seth than felt comfortable for two men. "You'll have to slum with me. What a disaster! Now we'll have four males and only two females. You expect me to make a change, too? You expect me to satisfy your brute sexual drive?"

His sarcasm wasn't truly joking. Reese Platte was older, around forty, with a worldwide reputation and an alphabet of letters after their name. They had won prestigious awards in astrobiology. They were rich — not in the same class as JC had been before he founded Mighty Mite, but they were not gambling their fortune on this expedition, as he was. Win or lose, Reese could go home to a life of unworried comfort. They considered Seth Broderick an uneducated young lout, kitchen help, the hand hired to do the heavy lifting. Reese, when female, was not the girl of Seth's dreams.

Wildcatters were notorious for promiscuity. Sex, after all, was what humans did, the one entertainment that never palled, and they were shut up for years at a stretch with no news of Earth, no outside friends, nowhere to go. Not all of *Hind*'s crew were equally lecherous. Hanna was puritanical and absolutely refused to play. Reese tended to cheat, being predatory when male and picky when female.

"That's your decision, Doctor," Seth said. "I do still hope to seduce you at least once before we get home." He was lying. He had no such ambition. She was twenty years older than he was.

"I admit I've been playing hard to get. Next time, I promise I'll take pity on you. But we may have to descend to this demon planet together, remember, and I don't think that such a dangerous situation is any place for a *girl*." He batted his long eyelashes.

It was true that a biologist normally accompanied a prospector downside, although only the prospector went outside. The bio stayed in the sealed, aseptic area of the shuttle. Somehow Reese staying in the comparative safety of *Golden Hind* had always been a more believable scenario. Now it seemed virtually certain, since Galactic had flagged Cacafuego as dangerous.

"It may not be any place for a man, either."

"But you will be so much more important to the success of the expedition," Reese said. "We can't afford to have you driven crazy by unslaked lust."

Seth leaned both hands on the back of his chair. "The mission is the only thing that matters, Doctor. If you think you will perform better under stress as a man, then keep your dingle dangling by all means. Don't worry about me. I have often gone months without being laid, I assure you."

"The Chinese would say that you need to conserve your yang for the difficult days ahead." Reese stalked away. Two pink pills a day and a high-fat diet would soon turn them female again, but even that medical miracle could never make them desirable.

⋆◦▬ ✴ ▬◦⋆

Seth went into the mess to clean up. It was longer than the control room and the absence of a central table made the curve of the floor more noticeable. It seemed smaller, though, because it was cluttered with comfortable chairs, fold-away tables, and recreational equipment. The floor and ceiling were currently displaying some arid Asian steppe with a camel train in the distance and snow-capped peaks beyond them. All these decorative routines were familiar by now; soon a troop of riders would start chasing gazelles along the stern wall.

Apart from that, the room was still in the shambles left over from the celebration. This was where Seth spent his days: here, the galley beyond, and on the hydroponics deck. Galley, mess, control room, sleeping cabins, showers, gym; those had been the crew's world for the last four hundred days. He also spent an hour a day exercising down on the 2-gee level, closer to the rim, where even running might break an ankle. He had been steadily popping pills to increase muscle and bone density until he could risk lifting weights down there now. Cacafuego's gravity was predicted as 1.2 gee.

Some law of nature decreed that the faster you traveled, the more boring the journey. Flying was less interesting than walking, and light-speed was the dullest transportation of all. For weeks the ship would drift in locator mode, seemingly motionless in infinite space, although in reality moving at huge velocity relative to almost anything else in the galaxy. Hanna had sent out unmanned supra-light-speed probes and scanned with dozens of instruments while everyone aboard fidgeted and fretted. Only when she, as navigator, had been satisfied that she had located another haven had she been willing to proceed. The jumps took no time at all, as far as human senses could measure. In one sense, they lasted negative years, for warping space also warped time.

He began gathering cans, glasses, empty plates, and full plates. What was he supposed to do with champagne bottles out here, hundreds of light years from the nearest recycling depot? His duties aboard *Golden Hind* were basically everything that nobody else wanted to do. JC had warned him of that when he hired him, fifteen months ago. Seth couldn't remember if he'd mentioned busboy.

DAY MINUS 47

046.12 Nothing in these Regulations or Ship's Rules shall be interpreted as requiring any member of the ship's complement to tolerate sexual harassment, or to engage in any form of sexual activity except voluntarily.

General Regulations
InterStellar Licensing Authority
2375 edition

⊷⊨◉ ⚹ ◉⊨⊶

Seth stepped out of the levitator lobby into Mighty Mite's offices, a reception area the size of a tennis court, luxuriously paneled with what looked like real wood but certainly wasn't. Huge, glaring pictures decorated the walls: galaxies a-twirling, bizarre landscapes from exotic worlds. None of them could relate to Mite itself, because the *Golden Hind* expedition was to be its first. Several doors might lead anywhere or nowhere; all were closed. The four young men sitting on couches around the walls were either his rivals for the prospector job or just decoration.

He waded through the carpet to the receptionist, who glanced up with eyes glazed by boredom. Skinny was the latest affectation of female young and she looked as if she had not eaten for months. Limp blond hair hung to her waist, and a blood-red Florenian orchid grew on the side of her neck.

"I'm Seth Broderick."

She corrected him. "You're Number Twelve. Take a seat until your number is called."

He headed to an empty couch. The most interesting thing in sight was a sign above the receptionist's desk reading: *Day -47.* Mighty Mite had still to finish hiring its crew, which was cutting it fine if it hoped to launch in a mere month and a half. The cost of building and outfitting a starship was literally astronomical, but if pressure from the creditors was forcing the pace, that would not reduce the risk any. *Has anyone seen the first aid kit?*

Without another glance at the opposition, he folded his hands on his lap, closed his eyes, and leaned back to seem relaxed. He had detected Mighty Mite playing mind games before, so he had no doubts that he was being observed; perhaps his heartbeat was being monitored. He had already noted that three of the four were sitting with eyes closed, lids flickering as they either read or watched some display visible only to them. The fourth was in the lotus position, which was definitely overdoing the icicle imitation.

There had been hundreds of applications, of course, perhaps thousands. He had endured three previous interviews and four medicals, each more thorough than the last, and now Mite had flown him to head office in La Paz to meet the great man himself. If JC Lecanard wasn't ready to make his decision by now, he was probably too inefficient ever to get his fogging ship off the fogging ground. Still twelve candidates with only forty-seven days left until launch? The presence of the others kept up the pressure on Seth, but some or even all of those four might be local actors brought in to play the part of additional candidates. They would be cheaper than plane tickets to Bolivia.

Three of the other candidates, or actors, were wearing formal suits, with calf-length pants, flared coats, and hats with feathers in them, as if they were bankers or lawyers. One of them was almost certainly a herm, although it was always hard to be sure. Lotus was dressed like Seth, in tank top, shorts, and sandals. That was all a guy ever needed these days, as long as he remembered to take a weekly sun block pill. Sun block pills were another exoplanet discovery.

"Number Fourteen," said the receptionist.

Seth opened his eyes. A door stood open. The possible herm rose, crossed the room, and disappeared. His calf muscles were impressive, but his hips were not true male.

Everyone went back to what they were doing, except Lotus, who hadn't reacted at all. No one had shown surprise at the number called, which either indicated that they already knew that the order was irrelevant, or else was a test to see if Seth could be rattled.

He closed his eyes again and sub-vocalized the code to check into ISLA's status page. It showed near-Earth space remaining quiet. *Golden Hind* was still in assembly orbit, together with two new keels, presently unnamed. Galactic had four in refit: *Bolivar, Courageous, De Soto,* and *Magellan.* Indra also had four: *Ganesha, Krishna, Shiva,* and *Rama;* but Indra was currently fully engaged in developing its world of Benares and would not be competing. Three of Bonanza's ships were due in from the Sagittarius sector within days: *Canopus, Polaris, and Sirius.* They would need time to refit.

So if a good planetary prospect was reported in the next couple of months, Mighty Mite might not face any significant competition for it.

After about twenty minutes the door opened again. Candidate Fourteen stalked across to the outer door, his face expressionless.

"Number Twelve," Anorexia said. None of the others squawked about having been there longer.

Seth rose and went to meet his destiny.

The CEO's office was even larger, the carpet thicker, and windows forming two sides displayed a magnificent view of a sandy beach with surf rolling in and palm trees waving their fronds about. Considering that Mite's HQ was on the forty-second floor, in the middle of one of the world's largest cities, which was itself 3,500 meters above traditional sea level, Seth was disinclined to believe that the scene was real. Besides, it would be centuries before sea level stabilized enough for mature beaches like that to form again.

JC was standing behind a desk composed of a slab of black granite floating in the air with no visible support. Was that symbolic of Mighty Mite's finances? He was dressed in a formal suit of white starsilk with a matching hat and a large black feather. He had large black-hairy forearms and was bigger than Seth had expected from his vid appearance.

He spoke his name, reaching a meaty hand across the desk to shake.

Seth spoke his, adding, "sir." Neither tried to crush fingers.

He was told to take a seat. He had a choice of one. Some hugely padded armchairs off in a corner were doubtless for informal chatting, but he didn't rank those.

On the far side of the desk, JC crossed his meaty legs and studied him for a minute or two. Seth studied him right back, noticing JC taking note of his arms and shoulders. Perhaps he should have worn long sleeves and long pants; in pink.

"Your resume is impressive, Broderick."

"Thank you, sir."

"Why do you want to venture into the Big Nothing, as we spacers call it?"

"To get rich."

"This will be a one-ship expedition. You know how risky those are."

"Yes, sir." On a ship-by-ship comparison, they weren't much riskier than fleet expeditions, but Seth was not going to argue with the Great Man if he said the moon was made of cheese.

"Your chances of surviving would be better if you signed up for a tour in downside duty on a development world, where the risks are known."

"Working for wages."

"Do you know the odds on a prospector surviving a first landing on a virgin world?"

"Yes, sir."

"You think you can operate coherently with that kind of risk hanging over you?"

"Yes, sir."

JC shrugged. "We're a start-up. You'd reduce your risk if you went wildcatting with Galactic or one of the other multinationals."

"Still for wages."

"Good wages."

Why waste time like this? Why not just tell him he was hired or kick his butt out the door? "Sir, I told you wrong. I don't want to be rich. I want to be filthy, flaming, fucking, disgusting rich. I want to be as rich as Drake when he took the treasure ship. You advertised a piece of the action."

"One half of one percent."

Seth managed to frown. "I was hoping for a full one percent." In fact a half was astonishing; he'd dreaded being offered a tenth of that. Risks had to offer worthwhile prizes.

JC shook his massive head. The feather waved. "Eighty-five percent for the sponsors, fifteen divided among the crew: five percent for me, three for the captain, and so on, down to the prospector, one half. That's still enough to make you a billionaire if we find anything worthwhile."

Seth shrugged and said, "That would do to start with."

"True, true! Old Mathewson used to brag that he'd built Galactic Inc. on one bucket of mud."

Seth smiled and nodded. Everyone knew that story.

The big man laughed. "He was lying! He brought back forty-three sealed vials of mud, dirt, water, scum, plant material, and pickled fauna. Forty contained nothing of any interest whatsoever. It was the forty-first vial that turned up the antimalarzine bacillus. Galactic was built on the profits from antimalarzine."

Seth tried to look impressed, but he'd known that, too, though. He had been working up to this day for more than half his life.

JC adjusted a pile of antique-style papers. "There are safer ways to get even filthy rich."

"I don't want safer, I want richer. We had a family legend about an ancestor who was a wildcatter when that meant someone who looked for oil. He struck it big and his descendants lost it all."

That drew a flash of interest.

"I've heard that before from people in the business. And 'prospectors', too — men who used to stake gold mines. Tell me more about yourself."

JC must have viewed at least three files of Seth telling about himself, plus his colonoscopy in living color.

"I was born on a farm in the New Desert." The rain had gone, the aquifers dried up, the soil blown away, and the temperature reached fifty degrees Celsius by midmorning, when the power went off. "When I was three my parents gave up the struggle and moved into town." City life had been even worse. He didn't say more about his parents — his father had worked a pedicab and died of a mugging when Seth was twelve. His mother had taken in laundry, succumbed to breast cancer three years later. The sister he had tried to raise had died of leukemia. When he reached his enrolment in NWTU, the big man barked a sudden question.

"Who paid for that?"

"I won a boxing scholarship."

"I understood that boxing was outlawed about the same time as gladiator shows."

Seth granted him a fake smile. "It's known as 'pugilistics' now and we fake the punches." Officially they did.

"You must have done well, to stay there four years."

"I was lucky. A lot of my opponents were very skilled at faking comas."

This time he got what looked like a real smile.

JC consulted the top sheet. "Astronomy, physics, sky-diving, karate, bungee jumping, gym, two medals in weight lifting, three in pugilistics as a lightweight, three more when you switched to middleweight, survival both tropical and arctic, hydroponics, domestic science, biology, organic chemistry, exogeology, exobiology, wrestling, pilot's license, history of space travel ... on and on. You never completed a degree."

"I hiked from school to school, taking courses from the best instructors — anything that might help me get into space, sir. I never failed a course. Prospectors need to be smart, tough, and fearless. I am smart, tough, and fearless. Plus I know a bit of everything in a pinch."

JC grunted. He was good, still giving nothing away. He would spring his traps when he was ready.

"I'm not allowed to ask you this, but I will. How's your sex life?"

"I'm straight," Seth said. "I avoid entanglements is all. I've wanted to get into space longer than I've wanted to get into women. I long ago decided I would never say, 'Bye, honey, look after the kids, see you in ten years.' I'm promiscuous when I get the chance."

"Never gay?"

"You're born with that," Seth said cautiously, "or not. I wasn't, but if I was with guys I liked and the nearest woman was a light year away, then I might get drunk enough. I don't know."

The big man's nod acknowledged a slick answer. "Fair enough. I'll be going along on *Golden Hind*, plus a crew of five. I wanted five herms, but there aren't enough good ones around. I've put together a first class crew of two women and two herms."

"I've had good fun with herms, sir. No prejudice."

"I still need a prospector. If I pick you, then you and I will be the only true males aboard. I don't want to have to fake a coma very often."

Wouldn't be hard to give him a real one. Seth judged that he could spot JC Lecanard a baseball bat and still take him in thirty seconds. But if JC fancied himself as stud male among five women or part-time-women, then pink might have been a very good idea.

"I expect you've gotten hold of my police record."

"That would be illegal."

"So?"

"It's clean except for a minor incident eight years ago. The court accepted your plea of self-defense."

"Which it was." Two muggers, armed with a knife and a shotgun. He'd knocked them both down and disarmed them, but one had claimed brain damage.

"You!" JC roared suddenly, "Are a fucking braggart, too fucking good to be true! I think half of this resume is bullshit. Get your ass out of here and stop wasting my time!"

His bluster impressed Seth no more than his palatial office. Big feathers make big birds.

"Well? What are you waiting for?"

"Your next question, sir. You didn't fly me all the way here to throw me out like that."

JC went back to the steady stare trial for a full minute. "It won't be fucking romantic, you know. Years of utter boredom, like time in jail. You'll be the gofer, bottom of the ladder. You do the housework, because we can't afford the fancy robots the majors take. You'll have machines to do the cooking, but you'll have to wait on table, load the dishwasher, pick up the laundry, clean the showers, tend the hydroponics. Are you man enough to be gardener and cabin boy, Seth Broderick?"

"Yes, sir." They knew from his resume all the things he'd done to pay for his education. They knew that even now he was a janitor by day, a bouncer by night, and taking a course in Advanced IT on time off.

The big man grunted again. "Any questions?"

"Tell me about Cacafuego, sir."

Big smile. "I know nothing about Cacafuego — yet. That's just Mighty Mite's own name for a target we still have to choose. All new data on exoplanets is funneled through ISLA, which saves it up until the final day of the month and releases it in one super news flash at midnight. Wildcatter ships stand by in dock orbit, waiting for it. If there's a decent lead they're off and running. If not, they wait for next month." Even bigger smile, even less convincing.

Seth nodded as if he didn't already know all that. The trick was to bribe someone to give you advance notice of next month's release. Or even two months ahead. Better still: buy data that never did get turned in to ISLA. It would all depend on how much you were willing to pay.

"If you do hire me, when do I embark?"

"According to the schedule, a week ago." Was that a deliberate slip, to make him overconfident? Or just a lie?

"What gear do I bring?"

"Your body and two kilos of anything you want. That's it. No drugs or crap like that."

"How is my share paid out? Who calculates it?"

A cloud-shadow of caution crossed JC's face; he leaned forward on his desk and seemed to choose his words more carefully.

"You get your share in Mighty Mite stock. We're a publicly traded company, audited, regulated, the whole shit. One hundred thousand shares authorized and issued. Five hundred shares will be registered in your name prior to departure and held in escrow until you return. Mighty Mite will make or break on this trip. The banks hold a ten-billion first mortgage on the ship and more than that in non-convertible bonds. If you can shovel up some useful crap for us when you go downside, we'll all be rich, and you'll get your share. Everything's aboveboard, no room for double dealing."

No? It wasn't how the rich got rich you had to watch, it was how they stayed rich.

"No more questions, sir." He had several, but none were deal breakers, so he needn't ask them. He was *almost* certain now that he had the job, but he wasn't going to let his guard down until he boarded. And not then.

"The first thing we must do is measure you for your EVA suits. How soon can you check in?"

Seth shrugged, mouth dry, heart beating wildly. "I'm yours as soon as I've read over the contract."

"No affairs to settle?"

"Nothing a couple of phone calls won't fix."

JC pulled an "I am impressed" expression. "Give me an access code."

Seth gave him a random number. "47746." He blinked and saw his com register a download.

"That's the offer and the contract terms. You have twenty-four hours, but I'd appreciate hearing sooner if you decide not to come. We have a coupla' thousand other candidates on hold."

"I'm a fast reader, sir. I can do it outside, there?"

"Of course." Lecanard stood up, displaying that ugly, unconvincing smile again. "There's nothing in there you won't accept.

I know a fanatic when I see one, and you'd sell your balls if that
was part of the deal. Welcome aboard, Mr. Broderick. You're a
real find! Glad to have you."

He held out a hand to shake. Seth saw the crush coming and
let it happen. It was bad. He didn't have to fake his yelp of pain.

One day he'd return that.

But he walked out of JC's office with his feet not touching the
fancy carpet. He had won his lifelong ambition, a trip into the
Big Nothing. He also had JC summed up as a bully, trickster, and
big-time operator, likely a crook whenever he could get away
with it. Hard and untrustworthy. A good man to have at your
side, never behind your back.

The receptionist had disappeared. The only other person in
the reception area was a youngish blond guy, probably a herm.
From the way his eyelids were moving, he was watching sports.

Seth took a seat and called up the new document. The contract
was shorter than he expected, because wildcatters basically sold
themselves body and soul for the duration of a voyage, subject
only to the ISLA's General Regulations, better known as the
GenRegs, and relevant Ship's Rules. A copy of those was attached
and contained no surprises that he could see. As he had expected,
anything he discovered, invented, or created would belong to
Mighty Mite, with the important exception of his prospector's
EVA log. When he had read everything he confirmed JC's sig
and Mighty Mite's corporate seal, then sub-vocalized his own
sig, and watched as it was verified. He copied the document to
his life files back in the New Desert E-Vault.

The blond herm must have been monitoring the Mighty Mite
end, because he jumped up and came striding over, offering both
hands and a huge grin.

"Welcome, Seth Broderick! Jordan Spears, captain of *Golden
Hind*." He did not try to squeeze. "Fergawsake, I bin sitting there
crapping bricks, terrified Old Ugly would turn you down."

Seth distrusted gushy offers of friendship. "Why would he?"

Jordan took him by the triceps and led him to the door. "Because
you're so screaming good! You should have seen the rest — trolls,
morons, and psychos. I am starving. You were the best by a light
year, but there was a shortlist of about thirty, any of whom would
have sufficed. Let's go and eat, and you can meet the crew."

"Why would he not take the best?" Seth asked as they left
Mite's offices.

Jordan smiled slyly. "Because you'll be the only other full-time male. Our beloved leader may not want any arguments about his leadership."

The levitator shot them up to a rooftop restaurant. Seth blinked at the first human waiters and white tablecloths he had ever seen outside a com show. He could see for a hundred miles; buildings and mountains, the curve of the Earth. He was on top of the world.

"This burger is on you?" he asked cautiously.

Jordan laughed. "It's on Mighty Mite, expense account. Table for five please, view of the sunset." The moment they sat down the captain ordered drinks and then sat back expectantly. "Feels good, doesn't it?"

How good could anything feel? Life's ambition on his first attempt? "There are no words for how it feels."

"Assuming you can sit there long enough to eat, what are you going to do to celebrate afterwards?"

"I want to go down to a gym and utterly destroy a punch bag."

"I went out and got myself laid three times in an hour."

"You're bragging."

"Sixty-five minutes, if you insist on accuracy. Want to try to better my record?"

Oddly enough, no. Sex, and especially the sort of trade sex Jordan was suggesting, would just cheapen Seth's sense of triumph. If he had a lover handy, that would be different. "I'll think about it."

"Fine. What do you want to know?"

Seth wanted to know if this was the end of poverty. He had just gone on expense account for the first time in his life. For several years he would not need to worry about his next meal. After that he might be astronomically rich, or back to flat broke. Or dead, of course. One chance in three wasn't too bad, and there were to be interesting side effects.

"I see from Ship's Rules that we're going monkeys, not monks?"

That won a wicked grin. "You're asking a herm? You know our reputation. Besides, what else do people do? It's the only universal recreation, rabbits in space... You don't believe me?"

"There's another universal recreation," Seth said, massaging his hand under the table. "A lot of people like to play power games."

"Some do," Jordan admitted with a genuine-seeming grin. "Not you or me, of course, but we both know one who does.

Yes, we'll do the monkey business. Statistics show that it works best. If you try to ban sex, it just goes underground and people get ratty. The only way to shut it down completely is to feed us chillers, but de-sexed crews get depressed, mistake-prone, and even more quarrelsome than when they're raunchy. Bed riding will be voluntary, of course, but chastity won't make you popular. You have a moral problem?"

A herm certainly would not. Herms were notoriously promiscuous. Herms needed to change over every few weeks, to avoid getting locked into one gender.

"Far from it. Who settles the arguments? If JC and I both want the same woman, or two women start fighting over me, who flips the coin?"

"I do. Lucky me. I don't have anything much to do with running the ship or exploring the planet. My job is the crew. I have to keep us all happy. I am authorized to try analyzing, tranquilizing, and screwing."

Seth chuckled. "JC fancies himself as an athlete?"

Jordan sipped his drink thoughtfully. "Maybe not. Two women, two herms, and two guys does sound like orgy week, but I think that one of the women is a bit of a prude and the other herm looks forty-ish, so we may be misjudging Old Ugly. He could have chosen better bimbos if that was what he wanted." Jordan smiled. "You hold four tickets in the lottery. I have five."

"So what's the rest of the talent like?"

"You'll meet them all in a few minutes. They're on their way." Jordan raised his glass for a toast. "Bon voyage and happy landings. May you become filthy rich and wallow in unheard of decadence all the rest of your days!"

"Same to you."

Looking into those laughing blue eyes, Seth realized that he was already being assessed as a future partner and that Jordan Spears must make a good-looking woman when they changed. She might not be as flirty then as he was being at the moment, but one of Seth's tickets looked like a sure winner.

He took another sip of whatever was in his glass. It tasted of sunshine and smelled like lithe young woman. "Do gofers get as much action as captains?"

"I wouldn't bet against it," Jordan said. "All cats are gray in the dark."

DAY MINUS 46

TO DAY MINUS 4

Dreams of colonizing planets of other stars are just that, dreams, and must always remain so. For the price of one starship you could build a city at the bottom of the ocean or a skyscraper on Mars. The only cargo that can ever justify the cost of interstellar transport is information.

Fonatelles, op. cit.

→⊨◎　✦　◎⊨←

Everything after that seemed like anticlimax. Yet time, which had crawled like a snail for months, suddenly went into hyperdrive.

The following day the crew flew to Space City to begin final training, and JC joined them there two days later. The mockup of the ship's living quarters was depressingly small, a claustrophobic line of windowless rooms no larger than a three-bedroom apartment. Seth had always been a solitary person, and the lack of privacy bothered him more than he had expected. He found himself due to share a room with First Officer Hanna Finn, a cuddly-looking redhead with a sharp sense of humor and an even sharper temper. She was the one that Jordan had called a prude, and she proved it the first night. There was nowhere to have a private chat with her ahead of time, a quiet sounding out of intentions. They would not be alone together until bedtime.

So he sprayed his teeth very carefully, shaved, washed, prettied up, and went to tackle the problem. The two single beds stood parallel, half a meter apart, leaving little space in the room for anything else. He closed the door on the world and the galaxy. She was sitting on the edge of a bed, reading — reading a real paper book, too! Seth had never seen one outside a museum. It must have used up a fair part of her baggage allowance.

He sat down on the other bed and leaned back against the wall. After a few moments she turned and frowned at him.

"What are you staring at?"

"I wasn't staring. I was admiring."

"And hoping, I presume?"

"Of course. But we can leave that until we know each other a lot better."

She snapped at him like a terrier. "No, it's something we can settle right now. I never engage in promiscuous sex. Carnal relations should be restricted to traditional marriage. Forget your lecherous ideas. The beds will stay apart."

"That's fine by me, ma'am," he lied. It had been a long time. She was a striking woman and he had been hoping. "Let me know if you change your mind."

"I will never change my mind. And I always read my Bible before retiring."

"What's your favorite bit?"

The big green eyes registered cynical disbelief. "Matthew, Chapter 5. You know it?"

"Oh, yes. Great stuff. I'm not sure I want to *inherit* the Earth though. I'm planning to *earn* it."

"Holy Scripture is not a fit subject for humor. Your ability to quote it isn't by any chance related to the fact that I left this book here earlier and it happens to open to that page?"

"Certainly not. My favorite is the bit in Paul's e-pistle to the Carthaginians about faith, hope, and love. Love's the greatest, he says."

"He didn't mean that sort of love, and he was writing to the Corinthians, not the Carthaginians."

Seth sighed and sat up to remove his tee-shirt. "As long as you don't do it aloud, I shan't complain." He preferred to sleep naked, but decided to leave his shorts on. Jordan had promised him four tickets to the lottery, but the first one he had drawn was not a winning number.

For the next five weeks the crew were kept frantically busy, spending hours every day in final training. Some of that had to be done elsewhere, so they were not entirely confined to the mockup, and could adjust to the cramped quarters gradually.

Seth earned his license on the hydroponic and synthesizer systems, and trained on a simulator until he was qualified to pilot an Oryo 9 shuttle. He was taught how to use the cooking machines, the cleaning system, and the laundry. He had to attend a general course on emergency procedures, et cetera, et cetera.

The end of the month came and ISLA's report included no new life-bearing planets discovered, which was a relief, in that *Golden Hind* hadn't missed anything. It was also a real concern. Accessible space was being mined out. Good prospects were becoming rare. The latest staking had been Munda Kmer, at 5,450 light years and almost thirty years' round-trip time, although that had included time slip, which might or might not repeat on a later visit. Many wildcatters were revisiting closer worlds that had been explored several times before.

Yet it was a real relief when news came that *Golden Hind* was ready for final trials. Next day they were hustled aboard a shuttle and blasted into orbit. For the three hours they needed to coast to docking point, they took turns at the port, watching *Golden Hind* grow and grow. Seth had seen plans, knew it would be shaped like a stubby carpet tack, with the discoid head being the ship itself and the shaft below containing the tachyon converter and the eight tokamaks that powered it. He had never guessed that it would be so big. Even Reese, who had done all this before and put on know-it-all airs, was too impressed to sneer much.

⊷⊜ ✳ ⊜⊶

The reality of *Golden Hind* itself gave him mixed feelings. JC's need for dominance, officially termed respect, was most obviously displayed in the sleeping arrangements. The commodore himself had a stateroom larger than the two other cabins put together. Three cabins, six beds. Hanna slyly referred to them as "our golden hindquarters."

Let the monkey business begin!

Seth, lowest on the totem pole, was appointed to the despised 02:00 watch and informed that the duty roster would not be changed during the voyage. Every spare square centimeter aboard was piled high with equipment and supplies that must be moved to permanent storage, largely by hand, and much of the storage

30

was down on the high-gravity levels. Guess who? The two space tugs made fast to the rim had just begun the long process of "winding up", so for the first week or so he had only partial gravity to deal with. That helped, but a fifty-kilo crate still had fifty kilos of inertia, even in microgravity. It took real muscle to start it moving and just as much to stop it again.

On the brighter side, he was assigned to share with dark-eyed Planetologist Maria Chang, a classic see-what-I-got-guys trophy: thick black hair, sultry black eyes, and a slinky walk that made his glands tingle. At first sight of all the females aboard, a man would instinctively choose her.

That first night, he retired early, which was understandable when he had to go to work at 02:00. He was awake when she entered. He sat up, bare-chested.

"Sorry. Didn't mean to wake you."

"I'm not sorry. Come here." He patted the edge of the bed.

"Oh, no! You think just because I have big boobs I'm a push-over, don't you?"

"I don't think any woman's a pushover; but we have months or years ahead of us here, ma'am, and I do hope that some time in the future we'll be lovers. Is that impossible?"

She tossed her head. "Perhaps not some time, but this is now."

He patted the bed again. "Come here, then."

"Why?"

"Because I want a goodnight kiss. Just one little kiss, I swear."

"Sure! And then one little caress on my breast. And you remove my top. And so it goes. And then, *bingo!*"

"Maria, I absolutely swear I just want one tiny little sisterly kiss."

She said, "Huh!" disbelievingly. But she did come and sit beside him, and he put a hand behind her head to guide her lips to his. He played fair, kept the other hand clenched. After the first minute she let his tongue in. After several more, she stroked his chest. So then he caressed her breast, she checked the state of his erection under the sheet — which was at warp nine, raring to go — so he removed her top. And so it went.

He must have acquitted himself well, because when he came off duty he found the two beds pushed together and her ready to go again. This was space travel as the legends had it.

⊷ ✳ ⊶

Time melted away. The critical end of the month was approaching, when ISLA would announce the next slate of candidate worlds discovered, if any. If they were ready, it would be up to JC and Mighty Mite's board of directors to decide if any of them was promising enough to be chosen as Cacafuego, *Hind*'s destination. If none looked good enough, they would set the clock back to *Day -30* and wait until the next month, or the next, or as long as it took. Still no other ships seemed ready to enter the race, but *Hind*'s good fortune could not last forever.

⊷━◉ ✲ ◉━⊷

Day -9 was memorable. The last cargo boat taxied Seth to the Oryo station so he could take delivery of the shuttle that would carry him down to the as yet unidentified world of Cacafuego. After signing for it, he flew it back and docked it in *Hind*'s only docking port, in the center of the disk. Granted that computers did all the work, that little jaunt made him feel like a real spaceman. After that there could be no further cargo deliveries, but the shuttle added to Seth's workload, because he had to check it out, inch by inch.

On *Day -6*, JC put them into overdrive, wanting to be ready to launch at a moment's notice. Seth, for one, worked until he was ready to drop. He couldn't see the urgency when no other ship on ISLA's list was spaceworthy yet, but he was willing to accept that JC had more information than he did.

On the evening of *Day -4* JC's voice summoned them all to the control room. He was beaming like a newly-fed tiger, clutching a piece of paper, but he said nothing until they were all seated. Then he waved the paper like a flag.

"This is it," he boomed. "The world of our dreams — Cacafuego itself. It scores slightly over nine on the Mew-Watson scale."

Pause for wild cheering. Niner worlds were rarer than snake feet these days.

"Only 1,500 light years away! In case you've forgotten, AKG's big strike is at more than three times that distance. The poor sods lost thirty-two years."

"Virgin?" Jordan asked skeptically.

"Absolutely. Its star didn't even have a catalogue number until last week."

"Why?" asked Maria, who was going to give Seth hell when she discovered the hickey on her neck. "Why should a world so Earth-like and so close — close by today's standards — go unvisited so long?"

"Weird sisters," JC boomed. "Other planets screwing up the Doppler trace. Also, it's in Orion. Dust clouds masking critical wavelengths."

"But not a new star?" Maria again. There was a lot of star formation in that area.

The commodore scowled at their skepticism and consulted his notes. "Right on the main sequence, type G. Metals date it a little older than Sol, but not by much. Why so glum?" He peered around and fixed on Seth as the safest target. "What's worrying you, sonny?"

"It's not the end of the month, sir."

"So?" JC demanded belligerently. "You look after the bug-eyed monsters and let me handle the politics."

"So you greased palms to get that information, but how do we know how reliable it is? Galactic has a fleet almost ready to launch. They might pay more than you just to have us sent off chasing wild geese."

The big man showed his teeth in a sneer of triumph. "You think I didn't think of that? I have backups. I put a lot of important suits on Mite's board, and two of them have checked out the coordinates for me, and they both confirm oxygen and chlorophyll lines in the spectrum."

This time even Seth joined in the roar of approval.

"There's also a bonus, of a sort," JC said, still riding his wave of triumph. "A backup I'm renaming Armada. It should be only two or three havens from Cacafuego. Not so promising, still in the slime stage. It's been staked before, but the claim will lapse soon, so I picked up an option pretty cheap. If we miss out at Cacafuego for any reason, we can go on to Armada and see if we can salvage something the finders missed."

Better still!

"Course locked in, sir," Hanna said quietly, and the babble died into shocked silence.

"Already?" Jordan exclaimed. "How did you manage that?"

The navigator looked smug. "The road to Orion is well mapped. There's a good haven at 213 light years, confirmed only four months ago."

"Then this is *Day 1*! Any idea how many days to target?"

Hanna took a few minutes, made more calculations. "There are listed havens all the way, but some haven't been visited for years and may not exist in our time slice. Allow a month or so to sound each one properly. There's lots of shoals around Orion, so we'll be zigzagging... Say *Day 425* as a best guess."

Jordan gave her a victory sign and turned to Seth. "Is the shuttle ready?"

"Yes, ma'am."

"You're sure? It's your lifeline."

"I'm sure."

"Anyone know anything that needs to be redone, rechecked, tied down? Nail clippers; bed socks; beads and mirrors for the natives? No? Very well." The captain laid both hands on the table. "Control, reset clocks to midnight, *Day Zero*. Launch Jump One."

DAY 401, CONTINUED

001.001 DEFINITIONS. The following terms shall apply in these regulations and any subsequent amendments thereto.

001.095 MASTER means the person in charge of a landing vehicle engaged in exploratory operations.

035.08 Notwithstanding anything else in these regulations, from the moment a landing vehicle disengages from its mother ship until it docks:

[a] the master is endowed with the autonomous authority of a starship captain,

[b] to be more specific, the master is not subject to the overriding authority of the mother ship captain, a ship commodore, or a flotilla commodore, as set forth in Sections 04 and 06, above.

General Regulations
2375 edition

Busboy-janitor-gofer Seth tidied away the vacuum cleaner hose, wondering as always if the system vented directly to space. Galley and mess were sparkling clean now, but he wasn't. He went along to the showers to wash his hands and scowl at his stubbled face and tousled hair.

Normally about this time he laid out dishes for breakfast and loaded the chefs with the correct materials, but he expected everyone to be late appearing today. He also had some questions to put to Control, which never slept, constantly gathering and collating data.

The camel caravan had advanced into the control room under a cloudless blue sky. Going to be fine day — that had been his personal joke for the last year.

"Whittington, I know you own the ship, but this is my seat." He scooped up the furry squatter and put himself between cat and chair. "Control, show me the hologram of the system again."

Camel steppe vanished and the planets appeared above the table as before. As sponsor, JC had naming honors, so the gas giant had become Hades, the two ice worlds Niflheimr and Jötunheimr, and Cacafuego's little satellite was Turd.

"Orbital parameters for the Cacafuego satellite, Turd?"

—*Preliminary estimates only, Prospector.*

"They'll do."

—*Mass 1.8 times 10^{23} kilograms... Semi-major axis unknown, current distance from planet...*

Smaller than Luna but at about the same distance. It would appear as only a very bright star and could not raise significant tides. Then came the data point he had been waiting for:

—*Inclination to the ecliptic, between 84° and 85°.*

"Stop. Have you estimated Cacafuego's axial tilt?"

—*Observations so far are too brief for an accurate estimate, Prospector.*

"Set limits."

—*Between 87° and 92°.*

So Cacafuego was a sideways world, tilted over, with its axis in the ecliptic plane. Worlds like that could grow ice caps around the equator, while the poles would have perpetual sunlight for half the year and perpetual darkness for the other half. Life might survive on such a world by hibernation or migration, but conventional theory held that advanced, multi-cellular life forms could not evolve there, meaning that the crew's dreams of untold wealth were doomed to disappointment. Even primitive slime worlds could provide interesting new compounds, but they rarely repaid their finders' costs or tempted people to go back for more.

Conventional theory often turned out to be wrong.

Any virgin planet that held life, as Cacafuego obviously did, was worth a visit when you'd invested trillions of dollars in getting to it. So why was Galactic planting warning beacons instead of staking it? Staking fees were nothing to Galactic, and if the initial samples failed to turn up anything interesting, the license could be sold to recoup some or all of the costs to date.

Permanent settlement of Cacafuego was not feasible, and never would be, and no one would ever want to colonize a sideways world anyway. Only the chance of finding exotic organic chemicals unknown on Earth could ever justify the cost of interstellar exploration. Curiosities like starsilk or the Florenian orchids that were the current fad in body decoration could be very profitable, but *Golden Hind*'s real hope was to take home a few liters of alien muck swarming with strange bacteria, spores, viruses, or whatever might be enough to make it a huge success. The yellow beacon meant danger, but an extreme axial tilt in itself brought no special danger, not in the short term of a wildcatter's visit. The climate might be a killer, but only over a course of months.

"Show me a blowup of Cacafuego."

The blue dot swelled, becoming gibbous, until it was about a meter wide, floating above the table like a grotesquely deformed balloon. *Golden Hind* was still three days out; Seth had not expected so much detail yet. He saw blue, with streaks and swirls of white cloud, shattered fragments of continent in brown and green. There was life there, much life!

The weather looked vicious.

"Climate?"

— *Terrestrial categories do not apply. The poles go from super-tropical to total darkness and back again. Islands near the equator appear to carry permanent ice caps.*

"Estimated gravity?"

— *Turd's orbit will soon allow a better estimate of the mass, Prospector, but we have already determined that the radius is smaller than first believed and the density abnormally high. Surface gravity is provisionally judged to be about 1.6 gees.*

Oh, balls! That was serious. He had been counting on 1.2 gees. He had worked for a year to add muscle and bone and succeeded so well that he had gone from middleweight to heavyweight, but on Cacafuego he was going to weigh almost 150 kilos, about twice what he had weighed back on Earth. How long could he function under those conditions?

"Why? I mean why didn't the trans-Neptunian observatories figure that better?"

— *The overall mass falls on their error bar, Prospector, but the planet's density is anomalous, meaning a shorter radius, and therefore the surface gravity is higher. Inverse square law,* Control added helpfully.

Seth called for animation, and was shown a few hours' rotation: a slow twist, then flip back, slow twist, flip back. Clearly the ship was approaching more or less along the ecliptic plane, aimed for about halfway between the planet's equator and the sunlit pole. Yes, there was ice at the equator. Some of that white might even be sea ice, which would make seasonal migration difficult for marine life.

"Latest estimate of the atmosphere?"

—Oxygen between sixteen and eighteen percent, balance nitrogen, neon, and water vapor. Sea level pressure estimated 1.7 atmospheres.

"Carbon dioxide?"

—Too small to measure at this range. Temperatures indicate it cannot be much higher than terrestrial, but there will be some, because there is chlorophyll.

His body could handle that air as long as he was allowed enough time to depressurize afterward. The oxygen content was lower than Earth standard, but that would actually be a blessing, because the partial pressure would be higher than terrestrial. If he had to, he could dispense with the EVA suit and just breathe through a filter mask to eliminate toxic dust and airborne bio-hazards.

Tiring of the endlessly repeated twist-flip, he called for a current view of the terminator at highest practical magnification. Like a view of the moon at the half, this gave him a sense of three dimensions, the mountains' relief being exposed by their shadows. The topography was Earth-like, suggesting plate tectonics, and that boded well for mineral distribution, soil fertility, and the development of life.

"Anything else unusual?"

The disk became an irregular, grainy detail. There was a coast, and an obvious river, and…

—We caught this by chance with our high-magnification scanner, and have not yet established a paradigm for the unusual texture. On Earth it would satisfy our parameters for provisional identification as a city seen in low-angle lighting, but there is too much vegetation to be sure at this distance and in this context.

Seth slumped back on his chair. *A city?* He was hallucinating, surely.

The rules for first contact overrode everything else, although they had never been applied in practice. Prospecting must cease at once. There must be no communication of any kind, only immediate withdrawal, leaving a beacon where the natives could not detect it. Events must be reported to ISLA, which would compensate the expedition for any financial sacrifice incurred, with a bonus. Plus historical fame to match Columbus's, of course.

"What color beacon for a sentient species?"

— *Purple.*

Made no sense! "And Galactic's is…?"

— *Yellow, Prospector, still yellow.*

"Holograph dismissed. Down on the floor, monster!" Seth rose and headed for the galley to flip some pseudo-eggs. The cat ran hopefully before him. He must be patient. In a couple of days everything would be clear. It couldn't be a city, just a trick rock formation. Evidence for intelligent aliens would certainly have sent the Galactic team high-tailing home to Earth with the news, but they would have posted purple, not yellow. He wasn't going to mention the shadows to the others. Let them find out for themselves.

But all that oxygen and blue water? Damn the little green men! Cacafuego was just too hot to pass up. The odds were very high now that in just a few days, Prospector Seth and Astrobiologist Reese would climb into the shuttle and go downside to that strange sideways world.

⊷⊷ ✻ ⊶⊶

After his usual solitary breakfast, he went back to the showers. He had just found his shaver when Jordan wandered in behind him, and for a moment their eyes met in the mirror. She had cleaned off the smudged makeup and brushed out the short golden hair, but she was topless. That was not unusual aboard *Golden Hind* and he was quite accustomed to seeing her naked in a cabin, a sight that never palled, but even semi-nudity seemed wrong under their present circumstances. She started at the sight of him and stepped quickly into a toilet cubicle. He went to the clothes bins, rummaged for top and shorts in her color, blue, and tossed them over the door to her. Then he went back to shaving.

When he was rich he would have his mess of a face tidied up. His nose had once been straight, his cheek had fallen in where he had lost four teeth to a lucky punch, and the too-recent scar on his forehead had come from a broken bottle. The wonder was not that he had only scored two out of four on the ship, but that such an ugly thug ever scored at all.

He had just reached the sandpaper on his chin when Jordan emerged, decently clad. No doubt she had started the change pills already, but no results would be showing yet. She was still a boyish woman with small breasts and narrow hips, but she excited him more than the voluptuous Maria ever did. He knew every pore in Jordan's skin intimately, the pink nipples and aureoles, faint pubic hair almost invisible against her pale skin. He hated the thought of those breasts shrinking even more, the slightly enlarged herm clitoris swelling into a workable penis.

He turned to face her as she came closer. Not too close, though.

"I screwed up tonight," she said.

Of course she had. The captain's job was to inspire the crew, which Jordan did with good humor and fine people management skills. Unlike Reese or JC, they phrased every order as a request and never pulled rank on the lowly gofer. The whole crew liked them, but no one doubted that JC had chosen Jordan Spears because they avoided confrontation. Unfortunately a face-off was sometimes necessary, and tonight the herm had blinked.

"No, you didn't," he said.

"Yes, I did. I should not be changing over."

He shrugged. "You made the right decision, love ... ma'am, I mean. No one knows more about fighting than me, and you never go into a fight with a monkey on your back. If you feel happier tackling Old Ugly as male, then you are quite right to change over."

"But it's a retreat, and he'll know it. Damn it, he can't over-rule me! He can't even overrule *you*, if you have good cause to refuse to go downside. I can handle that big ape without having to grow a cock. It's not fair to the others: you, Reese, Maria."

"Is he sane?"

Sidetracked, Jordan stared at him for a moment. "Be more specific."

"A trillionaire, sixty-two years old. What's he doing out here in the Big Nothing? Escaping from too many ex-wives?"

"Looking for the Great One, the world-shaking triumph to crown his career."

"And if he fails, he's busted. Loses everything. I worry a little about that." Was that true? Was JC sane?

"You could handle him if he turned violent," she said. "You're a fighter, an ex-bouncer. He's big but he's three times your age."

"The first time we met you told me I was the best applicant and yet you'd been frightened he wouldn't accept me. That why?

You thought he would red-pencil me because I could take him down?"

Jordan shrugged and put on her professional calming smile. "JC's not the type to go berserk, Seth. ISLA tests everyone for that."

"You're not the type to buckle under when a fat old bully shouts at you. Galactic's not the type to run away from danger. I sure as hell aren't, either. But I like to cover the bases. Let's talk about firearms."

Jordan nodded quickly, as if she'd expected the question. "All according to GenRegs. I have a stun gun coded for captain's use only. In the shuttle you have one plus a blazer, neither of which will work inside the ship."

"And JC Lecanard supervised the building of the ship. Don't tell me he didn't add a few little secrets. That champagne he produced last night wasn't in the manifest. Where's he got the guns hidden? Have you looked? Control tells me there aren't any."

"It tells me the same."

"But?" He knew her well enough to know that there was more.

Her smile was thin. "There's a table in his stateroom with a thick top but no drawer in it — wasted space. I can't find a hidden catch."

Seth desperately wanted to hug her. "Thank you ... ma'am." JC's big cabin was the one place he had never been inside and could never enter. All the others had, but the door wouldn't open for him. "Ask Hanna to take a look, mm?"

"I already did, love. Says she can't find anything either." Jordan spun around and walked away. She turned at the door. "I did make a mistake tonight. To reverse it now would make it worse. I'm sorry, lover, and I'll get back to you as soon as I can. You are by far the best stud aboard, you know."

That wasn't much of a compliment when his competition was two herms and a man forty years his senior.

→►○ ✴ ○◄←

By the time the crew trooped in for a breakfast, Seth had shaved and showered and dressed. Shorts and tops were color-coded, and his were green. The others were still looking more than a shade under last night's weather but too excited to sleep longer. Instead of eating in the mess, they carried their food into the control room to listen to Control's commentary and stare at the holographs while they ate. Maria guessed at the odd axial tilt the moment she saw the cloud patterns, which were all wrong.

Much jabber about sideways worlds followed. Apparently several planets with freaky axial tilts had turned out to be profitable, Lorraine especially.

Seth's excitement was back. Now he could admit that there was fear mixed in with it, but it was the thrill-fear he knew before fights, and it felt good. Having already eaten, he wandered around with the coffee pot, just listening to the chatter. Even old space hands JC and Reese were bubbling. Jordan seemed to have forgotten their worries for the time being.

He knew them all well by now and respected most of them very much. JC, Jordan, and Hanna were superlatively good at what they had contributed so far. JC was still a bully and insecure enough to demand formal respect, but he had done an incredible job in organizing the expedition, sneaking advance notice of the hot prospect, and ramming through the preparations in time to use it. He had even been shrewd enough to buy the Armada license as a secondary target, and few entrepreneurs would have managed to talk hard-bitten backers into that. Seth knew Jordan better than he had ever known anyone, and if it were possible to think of marriage to a herm, he would be dreaming of that now.

Hanna? Hanna was a brilliant navigator. She had a temper, but would always apologize ten minutes after losing it, and she had a needle-sharp wit. The other two had not had a chance to apply their skills yet. Maria he liked very much, and Reese he detested.

As a bed partner Maria demanded a lot of work and took sex too seriously. She was a fireball when she got going, after all the babble about respect and commitments. And yet, for sheer animal fun, Jordan beat her hands down. Random sex in so small a group should have triggered mayhem, but Jordan's skill and training kept them all one reasonably happy family.

Reese, the biologist, was the proof that every family tree has its sap. They were as snobbish as JC and as waspish as an August picnic. They were hypocritical, too. When male, he expected sexual favors, when female she refused to give them, at least to Seth, although JC claimed to have bedded her.

JC laid down his fork and put the planetologist on the spot. "Maria? Obviously there is life on Cacafuego. Nothing else could put that much oxygen in the atmosphere. So what can possibly have inspired Galactic to declare it dangerous and post a yellow beacon?"

She stabbed at him with eyes dark and dangerous as obsidian daggers.

"Radioactivity?" she said. "Cacafuego is abnormally dense, the second densest planet ever recorded. The core is denser than iron, meaning it must contain siderophile elements."

"You saying Cacafuego has a heart of gold?" Hanna inquired mildly.

"Gold is only one element that combines easily with iron. I was thinking of high-weight radioactive elements. If the core is rich in those, then we may expect to find such material in the crust also, exuding radon gas into the atmosphere, making it toxic to terrestrial life. Or the stellar neighborhood may be dangerous — there's an unpredictable Wolf-Rayet star within a parsec. Or the element mix at the surface may be non-standard: arsenic, cadmium are both toxic and carcinogenic, to name two. There are too many wolves in the forest to start speculating now, Commodore."

JC sank back, muttering that none of those factors would endanger a very brief visit. Given half a chance he might start retelling his story of the man-eating mushrooms found by *Goede Hoop*. "Reese? Any theories?"

At times the biologist seemed to hold the commodore in almost as much contempt as he did Seth. "Far too many. I could list a hundred factors that can create biological problems on a life-rich world. We don't have a canary with us. That's what prospectors are for."

Very funny! No one smiled.

Reese's sullen grumpiness suggested he was apprehensive — that was a snob word for scared. If Seth agreed to brave the killer planet, the astrobiologist should go with him. Failure to do so might void their contract. Or possibly Reese had decided to change gender and was already having changeover pains, for shrinking a penis by drug-induced apoptosis was no mean ordeal. Why would they do that now? Then Seth saw that JC might find it harder to order a woman into danger than a man. A sneaky cop-out, but only to be expected of Reese Platte.

As Seth was refilling his coffee cup, JC said, "How does it look to you now, Prospector? Think you can handle that 1.6 gee gravity?"

"Yes, sir. For a short stay. But the weather bothers me."

"Weather?"

"Storms. Dense atmosphere, high insolation gradient, fast rotation."

43

JC asked what the length of the day was, and Control became pedantic, as it did when human language was exposed as imprecise. The length of the day varied with latitude, for at the poles it was the same as a year, 250.3 terrestrial days. The sidereal period was 19.4 standard hours, so roughly 315 rotations per planetary year.

"Fast!" Maria said. "And high insolation because it's closer to its primary than Earth is to Sol. Is why it has all those cyclonic storms."

Reese barked, "Oh, damn! Control, what sort of surface winds do you calculate?"

—*Preliminary measurements suggest velocities in excess of 200 kilometers per hour are commonplace, roughly equivalent to Category Four hurricanes. Higher winds are certainly possible.*

"Ha! You can't put the shuttle down in that, can you, Muscles?"

"I can put it down, sir. Keeping it down will be the problem."

Reese pouted. At some time a surgeon had put a few tucks around their mouth. It looked fine when they were female, but their male lip curled in a perpetual sneer.

"By the way, the pH on the Number Seven hydroponic tank is low. I want you to clean it out this morning and bring up some lime for it."

"Sorry," Seth said untruthfully. "Can't."

The others were listening, and five pairs of eyes widened in surprise at hearing the worm turn.

He explained to Jordan. "Today I must make a complete inspection of the shuttle, ma'am. As soon as we have the planet's parameters nailed down, I'll have to start putting in hours in trainer mode, simulating flight in Cacafuego's gravity and atmosphere." He also needed hours of exercise in it, learning to walk, move, and hit targets with his stun gun.

JC leered.

Jordan bristled. The captain almost never showed anger, even when male. "On whose authority? I have not instructed you to prepare for downside activity."

"No, ma'am. But GenRegs say I must do so as soon as the target is sighted."

They also said that if, or when, that shuttle launched, Seth Broderick would hold the rank of master and be in effect commander of the expedition.

→► ✳ ◄←

Gravity in the ship came from its spin. By stopping the elevator at the right place between the axis and the outer rim, Seth could simulate any gravity from free fall to almost three gees. The shuttle port was up at the hub, the shuttle itself protruding from the disk of the ship like an axle. Not bothering with the elevator, he ran up the ladder. By the time he reached the top, he was in microgravity.

The shuttle was a delta-winged cylinder about the size of a city bus and it felt like home to him, his personal domain, where no one else ever trespassed. Access was by a shaft known as the Gut, which led upward from a door at the tail end. Currently the Gut was parallel to the ship's axis, so he floated along it with ease, going past the biologist's cabin, the Biosafety Level 4 laboratory, and the master's tiny cabin, to arrive at the nose, a nook known as the cab.

As he settled into the chair, Control activated the view screens for him. The ship spread out below him like a city plaza. Around the rim like pickets stood the ferrets, the light-speed scout probes, originally twenty-four, now only nineteen. Five had failed to return. Hanna suspected three or four of the remainder might be too badly damaged to use again, but it was better to scout out safe areas, the havens, with an unmanned probe than a manned starship.

"Initiate complete system check." He had run the shuttle through ISLA's entire inspection routine once a month since he left Earth orbit, being far more conscientious than the rules required, so he knew that it was in working order. Lights began flashing on the board.

— *Confirming complete system check, Prospector.*

Cacafuego glowed almost straight ahead, the way Seth was presently oriented, with its star blazing about ten degrees off to port. The heavens were rotating too slowly to notice. There were some very bright stars and emission nebulae in this sky. Orion was a busy stellar neighborhood.

That dazzling red disk must be Betelgeuse, a star larger than the orbit of Jupiter. Somewhere in roughly that direction, but much farther away, lay Sol and Home World. The thought made him feel painfully insignificant, out here in the Big Nothing. Not for the first time, he wondered why he was needed at all. The shuttle could be operated unmanned and robots could plant flags and collect samples just as well as any human being could. Primitive robots had begun surveying planets almost four hundred years ago. Once an exoplanet was found to contain exotic chemicals or useful life forms, almost all the development work of hunting for more was done by robots, with human overseers staying in orbit. So why did ISLA refuse to issue a development license without evidence of a human presence on the ground, however brief? The best guess was that the public demanded the romance. Prospectors were international stars. Seth Broderick and his like were the modern equivalents of gladiators, charioteers, or jousting knights, and they died to please the people.

—*Inspection completed. No issues to report.*

That had not taken long. Seth was not even being told to clean anything, although Control could be a worse hygiene martinet than a plague-year hospital matron.

"Prepare for simulated landing on world Cacafuego," he said, "using current best estimates of conditions. Assume winds of modal strength." He floated out of his seat to fetch the training suit, a sort of water mattress he could strap over himself in the chair. By pressuring that, Control could simulate the extra weight he would experience during acceleration. By the time he was ready, Control was offering him a partial map of the planet to select his preferred landing site. He chose an easy, flat area, well inland.

A full simulation would take hours, so he skipped the first three quarters of it. In a real landing he would have nothing to do except give directions at the end, picking a touchdown. Even then, Control would ignore his orders if they were likely to prove fatal. In this first simulation it slammed all the breath out of him in what felt like an impact with a granite mountain, then cheerfully announced that the shuttle had been smashed and he was dead. He was left feeling as if he'd been swimming in a cement mixer. He also felt very stupid.

"Let's try the last part again. From first atmospheric contact."

⇥ ✳ ⇤

"And again, but cut wind speed by fifty percent."

⇥ ✳ ⇤

At the fifth attempt, after he had reduced the wind strength by eighty percent, he landed safely, but he needed several more attempts before the simulated wind did not topple the simulated shuttle and roll it away like simulated tumbleweed. Wind was going to be far more of a problem than gravity. The shuttle ought to be chained down the moment it landed, and it was not designed for that. He had no tools to weld shackles to the diamond skin, and atmospheric friction would tear them off during the descent anyway. The shuttle could land on water, but that would probably be even more dangerous.

"How high do sea waves get here, within one kilometer of land?"

—Wave height cannot be measured directly at this range, and depends on too many parameters still unknown to estimate reliably, especially the profile of the shore. Higher gravity should reduce wave height but increase their kinetic energy. Terrestrial hurricane waves would be a useful first approximation.

Forget marine landing.

He called a halt. He was exhausted, soaked with sweat, and battered by Control's enthusiastic simulations. Small wonder: he had been in the cab for an astonishing ten hours. He shed the training suit and hung it back in its cupboard.

—First Officer Finn requests admittance.

"Open door!" He stared in surprise as the door slid aside and Hanna's green eyes and freckled smile came floating up the Gut to him. "To what do I owe the pleasure of this visit, my lady?"

"We began to wonder if you'd done a bunk."

He gave her a hand to steady her over the awkward threshold and turned the master's chair — the only chair — to her. She accepted it as a handhold but did not sit; he crossed his legs and floated in front of her. "Not yet," he said. "I'm an obsessive guy. Once I start doing something, I can't stop until I'm satisfied."

"So I've heard." That was as close to a mention of sex as he had ever heard Hanna utter.

Pity, that. Hanna still inspired fantasies. Jordan, that first day, had promised him four tickets in the lottery. Two of them, Maria and Jordan when female, had proved to be all a guy could hope for. Hanna and Reese were not even also-rans. They stayed in the gate.

"As a complaint?"

She ignored the question. Hanna was a puzzle. At thirty-two subjective age, she was slightly plumper than was fashionable but very comfy to look at. This was her second voyage into the Big Nothing. Her first had been a routine and uneventful return to a known world, but the ship had encountered some time slip and she had collected eight years' wages, which had made her independently wealthy. She was always gracious, although she had no use for stupidity. Normally she was so prim and reserved that she seemed almost stupid herself. In fact, she had a laser sense of humor, but most of her barbs would slip by unseen unless one watched for them. She was a genius at interstellar navigation, and when she said that Galactic must have cut dangerous corners to get to Cacafuego first, he believed her.

"Seth, dear, I came to remind you that the planet is still flying a warning flag. If JC insists you go downside and you obey him, Jordan and I will lose our licenses and ISLA will confiscate the Mighty Mite shares we hope to earn."

"I would never let that happen to you!"

"Then why are you wasting all day up here? Jordan cooked dinner for us."

Seth realized that he was starving. "What did she produce?"

"Chili con pseudo-carne, one of my favorites. I didn't know it was on the machines' menu."

"Because I don't like beans," he admitted. "But if there's any left, I'll make an exception."

She moved to block the exit and almost overshot it. "First tell me what you're plotting!"

"I plot not, Your Firstness." Private chats with Control did not count, and Hanna could command a replay of those if she wanted to pry. "JC was right in saying we should go in for a close look. Then we can work out what the threat is. Or let Galactic's beacon tell us, as it should do very shortly. I'm gathering information. After that we can make our own decision."

She stared at him suspiciously for a moment, and he sensed the penetrating academic mind she usually concealed. "You think you already know."

He nodded. "I've a theory. The weather down there is Satanic. Maybe Galactic lost a few shuttles and decided the grapes were sour. If that's all it is, then the only one at risk will be me."

"And Reese."

"If they want to come, yes." Seth still did not expect heroism from the biologist.

"Be honest. What are your odds of landing safely?"

"Not bad, if we pick a calm moment. I'm working on it."

Hanna smiled. "I know you are. Now come along. We saved some chili for you."

He straightened his legs, but continued to float. "Wait. You're rooming with JC just now."

Green eyes glinted. "Platonically, of course."

He couldn't resist the opening: "You mean he's impotent?"

"No, I do not! Don't you ever think of anything else but lust?"

"I just spent ten hours without doing so, and the strain is telling. I'm told that in JC's stateroom there is a table with a thick top but no drawer."

She waited, studying him. "And?"

"I suspect a secret drawer. I'd like to know what's in it."

"You want me to spy for you?"

"Yes, please."

"I wouldn't dream of it. What do you think he's got in there?"

"Weapons."

"No." Hanna pushed out of the chair and floated over to the door. "Come to supper…"

He caught her arm. "First tell me what he does have hidden in there."

"Porn," she said, turning away to hide her blush. "And stiffener."

➻ ✦ ☙

There was plenty of chili left. Seth took the whole pot plus a spoon and went into the control room. Everyone else was there, gathered around the console table. Above their dirty dishes floated Cacafuego, ballooned to about two meters. Half lit, half dark.

He was greeted with welcoming smiles from all except Reese, who despised people who ate out of cooking pots, which was probably why Seth was doing it.

"Hanna tells us you can land on the planet!" JC boomed.

Seth nodded with his mouth full and sat down. He didn't mention how risky it would be. Maria filled up her empty glass with red wine and pushed it over to him.

Between mouthfuls of chili he said, "What's new?"

"It's mid-July in the northern hemisphere," she said. "Roughly, it is. We're calling that side north; it's pretty arbitrary in this system. But the axis is still pointing almost directly at the star, so the other hemisphere is in darkness."

"Overall it's a hot world," Jordan said. "Permanent ice on most equatorial landmasses; a lot more ice in the southern hemisphere, but that's seasonal. That big island near the north pole — JC's named it Greenland — is reading more than fifty degrees Celsius in the shade."

Reese next: "And the only shade is under trees, if there are any trees. Unending sunshine for about half the year; humidity close to a hundred percent. Oh, the biota that baby must have!"

Jordan called for a map. The globe projection became cartographic, with green, brown, or white lands in a uniform blue ocean, names in black. Clouds and the day-night distinction vanished. About a third of the southern hemisphere had not yet been visible to *Golden Hind's* sensors, and remained blank. Most of the world was ocean, more than Seth would have expected — he would have to ask Maria about that. Small equatorial ice caps were starkly obvious.

Voices began arguing about landing sites, gloating over the prospect like children in a toy store. They were all assuming that the shuttle could meet its design parameters, going downside twice, visiting four sites each time. Seth knew otherwise.

He must catch some sleep before he was due on watch. He finished the last of the chili, drained the wine, and began collecting plates. When he tried to take Reese's glass, the astrobiologist grabbed it away from him and pulled the bottle to safety too.

"This happens to be a perfect Feigned 2223 *Chateau Lavoir* classic Bordeaux! It cost hours of simulation. It is to be sipped and savored, not swigged like some ghastly cola." Even Reese was rarely so bitchy. The knowledge that he might have to go downside on an allegedly killer planet must be working on his nerves.

Seth shrugged. "It all comes out of the recycler. I pissed it four days ago." He was letting the sneers get to him, but in his case that was due to excitement, not fear. The difference was quite obvious, at least to him.

DAY 404

Prospectors are the wildcatters' heroes, but prospectors' heroes are the first-footers, the select few who have been first to step out on a new world and stake it. I once met the legendary Gabriel Leigh Sullivan, who did that six times and lived to a ripe old age. I asked him how it felt.

He said, "Addictive."

Fonatelles, op. cit.

⊷⊨◉ ✦ ◉⊨⊶

The next few days flashed by in a fog of too little sleep and far too much work: simulated landings, high-gravity exercise, and cleaning out hydroponic tanks to ensure that the system would survive his absence — provided that his absence was brief. If he did not survive, then dear Reese would have to take over the gardening. Seth also had to haul biological supplies up to the shuttle from refrigeration on the storage deck. Nobody offered to relieve him of any of his regular duties.

That evening, ship time, Jordan called yet another conference. The captain had completed their change, and was now back to being the slim golden-haired young man with blue eyes and a big friendly grin whom Seth had first met in La Paz. Their exceptional good looks were more noticeable when they were male, verging on the angelic, but it was impossible to dislike Jordan in either gender.

"Meeting come to order, please. In about three hours Control will stage a micro-jump to shed velocity and enter orbit, unless we decide that this world is hopeless. In which case we set course for Armada instead." He shot an amused glance along the table to Seth. "Prospector, you have not reported on the results of your landing simulations. Not a peep."

"No, sir. I lost track. Control has a better memory than I have."

"Control, report."

—*Landing simulations directed by Prospector Broderick: twenty-four, with three, or twelve percent, successful. Simulations without human input, two hundred and five, with thirty-one successful, fifteen percent.*

"Shit!" The vulgarity came from JC, predictably.

"I second that motion," Jordan said. "Or do I mean movement? When does courage become insanity, Seth?"

"Somewhere between a barrel shop and Niagara Falls," suggested Reese, looking relieved. To Seth's astonishment, they were now female. Even sharing a cabin with them, he had been too exhausted to notice the switch. Was this just because they thought Jordan would consider it unchivalrous to order a mere woman to go downside? As a herm themself, Reese ought to know the captain better than that. So why?

"I will not allow Prospector Broderick to attempt a landing on this planet," Jordan announced. He glanced at JC's thunderous frown and then ignored it. "Under the circumstances, I see no need to continue radio silence. Control, have you found any evidence of Galactic's fleet, or of any other ship in the vicinity of this planet?"

—*None except the beacon, Captain. Its timer indicates it was activated eight terrestrial days ago.*

That had been only four days before *Golden Hind*'s last jump. Activating the beacon would likely have been the last thing the Galactic fleet did before departing the system, so *Golden Hind* had probably not lost the race to Cacafuego by more than two or three weeks, and their time slips must have been roughly equal.

"Is the Galactic beacon emitting any verbal or visual message?"

—*No, Captain, but its signal indicates that it will do so if queried.*

Both hands on the table. "Overriding previous orders, break radio silence. Query the beacon for us."

A man of lined face and graying hair appeared in head-and-shoulders holograph. He wore a blue shirt and a raddled expression. He looked steadily into Seth's eyes, and into everyone else's too.

"I am Madison Duddridge, commodore of Galactic Inc. expedition GH796 and captain of exploration vessel *Bolivar*."

People called Madison were usually herms, but he had a bass-baritone voice and shaggy eyebrows.

"We are posting a warning beacon on this planet, ISLA reference GK79986B, provisionally named Hesperides by us. It is our sad experience that this world is too dangerous to explore. Surface temperature varies from above 50º Celsius to below minus 90. The weather is violent and beyond the ability of our computers to predict on the data presently available. We sent down many unmanned drones and all of them crashed in less than an hour."

Golden Hind carried no atmospheric drones, only deep-space probes.

Duddridge still looked earnestly into Seth's eyes: See how honest I am?

"In the belief that a larger craft would have a better chance of surviving, three very brave people agreed to go down for a brief reconnaissance. They were Prospector Meredith Tsukuba as master, Prospector Dylan Guinizelli, and Astrobiologist Mariko Seidel. Their chosen destination was a site we called Apple, on an island we named Sombrero, at latitude thirty-one north, counting north as magnetic north, in the approximate direction of the blue giant Bellatrix. The climate there appeared to be relatively benign.

"They landed safely. The two prospectors made a brief excursion, collecting preliminary samples in case they had to depart in a hurry. In the brief time they were absent, a stray gust of wind damaged their shuttle. Both Meredith and Dylan, caught out in the open, were thrown down and he broke his arm. Meredith helped him back to the shuttle, where Mariko tended him in quarantine, in case his suit had been compromised by the fall.

"Within hours, Dylan developed a high fever. He subsequently went into coma and died. Later the two women became sick, suffering fever, hallucinations, and intermittent coma. The unknown pathogen must be extremely virulent. Moreover, the women insisted that Dylan's EVA suit had not been compromised, and he was kept in strict quarantine until Mariko also succumbed. The infective agent is thus capable of penetrating the best biosafety barriers modern science can provide.

"As soon as weather permitted, we sent down a second shuttle, unmanned. Again the weather foiled us, and it crashed about a kilometer away from the first."

The speaker paused as an indication that the news was about to get worse.

"You certainly spotted the tiger in that jungle, Seth," JC muttered, being unusually gracious.

"The first shuttle suffered additional damage by winds of major hurricane force, which rolled it. After that, no further signals were received from the ground party. I regretfully concluded that they had perished. Prospector Tony Violaceus, from the aptly named *Courageous*, very gallantly volunteered to take down a third shuttle in a rescue attempt. I refused his offer.

"We are therefore mourning all three of our comrades as lost, and posting this warning beacon. We expect that ISLA will declare Planet GK79986B off-limits, and you will find it so listed in the catalog. Of course, if this message is less than twenty years old when you receive it, we may not have returned to Earth in real time prior to your departure, and I can only urge you to heed our warning and learn by our tragic example.

"Again I honor the names of Dylan Guinizelli, Mariko Seidel, and Meredith Tsukuba." The image disappeared.

The silence grew cold as everyone waited. Cue the violins.

At last JC said, "Tsukuba was our second choice for prospector after Broderick."

Seth had not applied for the Galactic post. That would not have been him down there.

Jordan said, "Their story sounds pretty convincing to me, JC."

Mr. Money was harder to convince. "Flaming pig shit, is what I'd call it, Captain. Galactic normally sends out a flotilla of three ships, which can hold twenty-four hour full-spectrum surveillance of any given location. Each ship carries at least one shuttle. Seth, lad, if you'd been there, would you have made the same offer that their Tony character made?"

"I hope I would, sir." Seth kept his face dutifully serious, but he was amused. The campaign to win over the heart and mind of Prospector Broderick had begun.

"And would you have refused, Captain?"

Jordan pouted. "I am very glad that I didn't have to make that decision." He never would, because *Golden Hind* carried only one shuttle.

"But if you did?"

"I think I would have let him try, probably."

"Course you would," the commodore said. "But Galactic's crews are paid wages. They're not motivated to hazard their pretty necks the way we are, as shareholders."

Some necks were motivated a lot more than others, in Seth's opinion, but that had sounded like a faint offer to renegotiate a vertebra or two. It was also a flat contradiction of what JC had said a few days ago, when he had accused Galactic of recklessly risking the lives of its employees.

Reese said, "It's a two-headed tiger now, sir. First the weather and now this mysterious poison or infection."

"Don't eat that stuff. Infection will be no problem as long as you observe standard rules, like over-pressuring, and maintain asepsis. The damage to the shuttle exposed them to infection."

Maria said, "Sounds like they had no time to analyze anything. Even the drones brought back no samples."

"Maybe not," JC said. He was angry and defensive. "Or maybe. The downside lab could have reported more than we were told. A really deadly airborne poison would be a big seller back home. Governments—"

"*No!*" Jordan snapped. "Let's not descend to peddling death."

Surprise gave way to amusement at his returned assertiveness. JC's shrug conveyed indifference. He knew, as they all did, that the contract did not distinguish between ethical and unethical discoveries. Only very rarely could wildcatters be sure what they had found until it had been analyzed in terrestrial laboratories. Almost anything could be turned into a weapon.

After a moment Reese said, "Galactic is rarely troubled by scruples. Even if they knew there was a bio-weapon there for the taking, they haven't staked the planet."

"They couldn't! That's obvious!" JC barked. "No footprint, no claim."

"They scared off very easily," Hanna said. "They may not have told us the whole story."

"Of course they didn't. Galactic never does. Well, Captain? So they lost three hands. Tragic. ISLA will review their records and hold an inquest. But who's to say they don't plan to build a tougher shuttle and come back? Technically it wouldn't be difficult. Galactic can afford it."

That made sense. Seth wondered how the story recorded on the beacon would relate to what was reported to ISLA. He even had a far-out idea of what might have killed off the Galactic people so rapidly, but it was a theory that ought to have occurred to either Reese or possibly Maria, and he wasn't about to throw it out in public yet. They might be deliberately not mentioning it.

There had been some very odd things in Madison Duddridge's story. The shuttle was damaged. *De Soto* sent down another. It crashed. A storm blew in … and that was that. How long did the storm last? Closer to hours than weeks, because those mothers were ripping around the planet like swallows in mosquito season. Galactic must have instruments that could see through rain, that could certainly identify the shuttle and probably even individual people. So why not send down a second rescue mission? The storm might have wrecked the shuttle's antennae, but why abandon two people who might still be alive? The thought made him boil.

Jordan called for more suggestions and no one spoke. "Very well. The question is whether we stay to explore this planet from orbit, with no obvious way to attempt a landing, or whether we proceed to Armada. By law, the final decision must be mine. I am strongly leaning to the Armada answer, but I invite comments."

"I think the decision should be the prospector's," JC said. Eyebrows rose all around the table. "If he isn't willing to go downside under any circumstances, we can do no more good here than Galactic has already done. If he thinks there's a chance, then we owe it to ourselves and his courage to spend a week or two here."

Seth also heard, *And we might be willing to bribe him a little.*

The captain looked along the table to Seth. "Prospector? At the least your voice must carry more weight than anyone's."

"Sir, I'm not quite ready to say it's hopeless," Seth said. "We've spent fourteen months getting here. Captain, I agree with Commodore Lecanard that another weekend won't hurt."

Jordan studied him suspiciously. "You'd make a landing against those odds you gave us?"

"No, but I think I can cut those odds now, sir. Control, report the results of the last thirty simulated landings."

—Most recent thirty landing simulations, twenty-three successful, seventy-seven percent.

"Well that settles it!" Jordan said. "Those odds are not—"

Seth had raised a hand to stop him. "Control, report the results of the last twenty simulated landings."

—Most recent twenty landing simulations, eighteen successful, or ninety percent.

JC was starting to smirk. Not much got by him.

"Report the results of the last ten simulated landings."

—Last ten landing simulations, one hundred percent successful.

JC roared in triumph and beat his fists on the table.

Jordan's eyes burned like blue lasers; he was angry at being tricked. "How did you manage that, Prospector?"

"I cheated, sir. I need more time to make sure the cheat will work in practice."

"I'll accept that. You're due on watch in a few hours and you look like you haven't slept in a week. The rest of us aren't helping you enough."

Seth just shrugged.

"From now on you are relieved of all scheduled duties. I'll post a new roster for the rest of us. You concentrate on the prospector duties. Control, enter orbit as proposed. Reese, clear away the dishes, please. Seth, I want a word with you."

—⊙— ✳ —⊙—

Jordan strode down the corridor to his cabin. Seth followed him in and closed the door.

"Sit!" Jordan pointed to the only chair, vaulted backwards on to a bed, and crossed his legs. Seth sat and laid one ankle on the other. His eyelids weighed tons. He had been working fifteen hours a day and not sleeping well the other nine.

"I can guess what you're up to," the captain said, "but it won't work unless you promise him you'll try a landing."

"That's what I'm working on, sir."

"Can you drop any hints?"

"No, sir. I won't know until Control can tell us more about conditions downside."

With obvious disapproval, Jordan said, "Ok. But I warn you, if I think a landing looks too risky, I won't allow it, no matter how much JC screams and yells. Now, listen. What I want to talk about … I know you desperately need to go and exercise your snoring muscles, but what I really need to discuss is you and Reese. You're snapping at each other again."

"I'm sorry. I—"

"No, it's understandable. They call you dirty names and put you down every chance they get, whichever gender they are. It's worse when you have to share a cabin. Do you know why they changed back to female again this time?"

"In case I do take the shuttle down. So you won't make her ladyship risk her pretty little ass."

Jordan smiled and shook his head. "No. She's probably risked it in worse situations. Down, boy. I need to tell you a few things about Astrobiologist Platte."

Seth crossed his ankles again. He didn't need sex at the moment, or even talk about sex, just sleep. Hours and hours of sleep. He worried about letting the others down, letting himself down, muffing the only big chance he would ever get. If he went back home without trying the Cacafuego landing, his prospecting career would be over. No other expedition would ever hire a proven quitter, and he would never forgive himself. But he mustn't let wishful thinking lull him into stupidity. If he tried and failed he would leave *Golden Hind* without a shuttle, so the others would have no choice but to head home again, with their hopes in tatters. What was the question again?

He thought back over the voyage. "You've been roommates twice?"

"Yes, but never this way round. Male, Reese's a competent stud, a bit predictable but patient and gentle. We've agreed that next time we'll change ends. You know how old they are?"

"Forty-one?"

"Older. But that's subjective time. This is her fourth trip into the Big Nothing. She was born in 2282, ninety-four years ago. About seventy years before you were."

Seth had no answer for that.

"They were one of the very first herms, Seth. Their family was wealthy, old money; their father won a Nobel Prize for medicine. Can you imagine a man who would put the experimental herm drugs into his own pregnant wife? Reese was conceived as a boy, if that matters to you. The process worked without a flaw, but they were a freak in their childhood, mocked, toured around like a circus. And their father was an absolute martinet, a disciplinary extremist. I gather their mother was a Marie Antoinette-level snob."

"Tragic. Which part of this does she blame on me?"

"Seth, Seth! She blames herself. Raised by a tyrant, brought up in a mansion, taught to despise the lower classes and their lustful debaucheries — you know how priggish people were last century! Now, thanks to some time slip, she's lived so long she finds herself in a whole new culture, and she goes and falls for an uncouth, uncultured, muscle-bound, penniless yahoo a quarter her age?"

Jordan leaned back on his elbows and grinned at Seth's disbelief.

"It's true, Seth! What they tell you isn't what they mean at all. Imagine how ashamed they feel. I don't think they changed over this time because they were worrying about accompanying you. She just wants a few nights with you before you leave."

"Nights to do what, fergawsake? Call me dirty names?"

"To get raped," the captain said softly, and laughed at Seth's reaction.

"Never!"

"I'm not suggesting you do it. That's up to you. I'm just explaining that that's the role she sees for you — a boorish, foul-mouthed, bodice-ripping punk imposing your lustful demands on her, ordering her into bed, talking dirty."

Seth swallowed and licked dry lips. "You are telling me that Reese Platte has rape fantasies?"

"When female, yes. And you are the thug of her dreams."

"You can't order me to do this."

"Of course not! But every mind has a few dark corners, Seth, and that's Reese's. She desperately wants you to call insult her, tear the clothes off her, even slap her around a bit, and then overpower her and screw her. She'd weep with joy. If you can't fit the pistol, at least try to be understanding."

This conversation was downright unbelievable. Jordan had a string of degrees in psychology and was licensed to practice in three states. He would never gossip about another crew member's emotional problems. So what was going on?

Seth stood up. "Captain Spears, sir, I cannot do things like that. Not hurt a woman. Not even under orders. You shouldn't be suggesting such things. Shit, I had a kid sister I tried to rear. I watched both her and my mother dying in agony. I cannot do what you or Reese want. If I want violence, I go to the gym, pick out a guy who outweighs me by twenty kilos, and beat the hell out of him."

"I'm not ordering you; I am merely explaining why you have problems with Dr. Platte."

"No, sir. If she has problems with me, tell her she can ask me herself. And there will be no rough stuff."

Seth stalked out, shaking his head. He wished he hadn't been told all that. He really had no desire to lie with a woman of ninety-four. He took a long, soothing shower and sprayed his teeth. Then he headed for the cabin. It was dark, but light from the corridor showed him that both beds were empty, which was a huge relief. He fell into his with his clothes on and barely had time to order the lights off before he was asleep.

DAY 410

Back when astronomers knew only the solar system, they tended to assume that the sun must have collected a complete set of possible planets. Now we know better. Now any wildcatter will happily quote "Blackadder's Law" for you. Credited to Nicholas Blackadder, one of the early interstellar explorers, Blackadder's Law states simply, "Every world is different, except that they're all out to get you."

Fonatelles, op. cit.

⊷═◉   ✳   ◉═⊷

Jordan convened yet another meeting, this time to consider whether to continue surveying Cacafuego or set course for Armada. This was the showdown, and Seth knew that his decision would be crucial, although he might well be overruled in the end. Everyone knew the stakes. He kept catching sideways glances, appraising him, wondering which way he was going to jump. He wasn't sure of that himself.

The big change showed in the way they sat around the control room table. Although their positions were still the same, the balance of power had shifted, from the three at the far end who had brought them here: commodore, captain, navigator, to the three whose job had now begun: biologist, planetologist, prospector.

Large-scale maps of the planet filled the control room walls, showing the daylight hemisphere and the ever-moving ship's icon. No sign of the Galactic fleet had been detected. Its quarantine beacon flew a high orbit that should be stable for centuries.

"First," Jordan said, "a quick recap of what we know, so that we're all on the same page. Maria?"

"Cacafuego's high gravity is actually helping us now. It compresses the atmosphere, so *Golden Hind* can orbit close in without experiencing significant drag. We have five ferrets in orbit, and they're mapping on a low-detail scale. Of course we would need months to analyze all the scattered land masses, but we can examine narrow strips in very fine detail. Certainly there is life down there, as Reese will tell you — advanced, multicellular life. We've seen forests and savannahs, and marine fauna as large as whales. No large terrestrial animals yet, which suggests that the year-long cycle of day and night inhibits their development."

"Elephants don't hibernate well," Reese said.

"Or migrate across oceans."

JC said, "Maria, run through this sideways climate scenario again for me. It drives me schizo."

"Don't you mean bipolar?"

A blend of groans and laughter broke the tension.

"Kill her," Reese said.

"Ok, ok, I'm sorry. Imagine you live at the north pole. At the summer solstice, what we'd call roughly the end of June, the sun stood directly overhead all day, meaning about nineteen terrestrial hours. The heat is super-tropical, too hot for any terrestrial life other than some extremophile bacteria. Now the sun is descending in a spiral. If you're exactly at the pole, the spiral will be symmetrical. By the equinox, the end of September, it will make a daily run around the horizon. A couple of days later it will sink out of sight for half a year and the temperature will drop far below zero.

"Now suppose Hanna lives at the equator. She sees something very different. At summer solstice the sun is due north, motionless at the horizon, or a fraction above it because of atmospheric diffraction. In this perpetual dusk, the weather is bitterly cold — arctic by our standards. Slowly the sun begins to move in increasing circles, gradually tilting so that each day it rises higher. The circles grow until, at the equinox, it rises due east of you and sets due west, passing directly overhead at noon. Then the days shrink again. Got it now?" Maria glanced around the table.

Heads nodded.

"In the spring, the sun does the reverse, except that it rises in the west and sets in the east."

"She's making this up," Seth said.

"I am not!"

"I know you're not. Tell us about the weather."

"Loads and loads of weather! Right now the air in the northern hemisphere has spent half a year above a super-tropical ocean, which must get dangerously close to boiling near the pole. The air is hot and saturated, hurricanes are two-a-penny. In fact some of them may be close to permanent, whirling around the globe. The southern hemisphere air is super-arctic cold, and at this time of year the two bodies of air are starting to mix as the sun rises over the equator. The temperature difference could easily top a hundred degrees Celsius. You wonder there are storms?"

"And what about tides?"

"Tides? Um, I haven't thought much about tides yet," Maria admitted.

Seth had. "Turd is too small to raise much of a tide, but the sun must. And it must pull a lot of water to the poles at the solstices, big stationery bulges. By equinox the tidal bulges will be sweeping around the equator. So getting from one state to the other must be quite exciting at times."

Everyone looked at the maps. Cacafuego had at least eight mini-continents and many smaller islands. Some places must see huge tidal surges at those times.

Maria said, "Control, estimate tidal range at Sombrero."

—*Zero to approximately ten meters, depending on season and not allowing for storm surges.*

Seth had already asked Control that, so he was not surprised. The others obviously were. It was another factor to take into account.

"Any more questions on the climate?" Jordan asked. "Control, show us Sombrero again. There. Thirty-one degrees north latitude, about the latitude of Jackson, Mississippi. It fits Commodore Duddridge's description, although I'd call it a small continent."

Whichever it was, Sombrero had a central plateau and a couple of curved coastal ranges. With some imagination it could be seen as a very battered and lopsided Mexican Hat. Jordan ordered a blow-up, but yesterday everyone had been shown what was coming next. The world maps faded and Sombrero swelled to fill the walls. Most of the image was grainy, but a few strips of better detail happened to have caught the evidence *Golden Hind* needed. A flashing circle highlighted one pathetically small white shape.

Jordan said, "Control has identified this as a crashed shuttle, to a confidence level of ninety-six percent. It is too large to be a robot drone, but we cannot be certain yet that it is Galactic's manned effort. It could be the unmanned rescue attempt that crashed 'about a kilometer away' but we cannot find a second wreck. This is the site they called Apple. Maria, do you want to comment on the location?"

Maria did, but at first she said little that Seth had not worked out for himself, or obtained from Control. The Galactic landing was a few kilometers from the sea, on an expanse of sandbanks and green islands that looked like a wide flood plain. The river itself was broad, flowing eastward from the central highlands. JC had already named it the Tsukuba, after the master of the crashed shuttle.

"Apple was a good choice for first touchdown," Maria said. "The climate is bearable at this time of year. At midsummer it had permanent daylight, but not too hot, with the sun staying about thirty degrees above the horizon. Now it rises a few degrees higher than that at noon — higher every day — and dips very close to the horizon at midnight.

"It has river, swamp, and grazing land, whether grass or not. No forest, but several environments to sample. And some odd-looking rocks. According to Control's estimate, based on their shadows, they're about ten meters high, roughly conical, with truncated tops, possibly open, although we can't be sure of that."

The crashed shuttle was so close to the rocks that they must have been the primary objective. They were not the same features that Seth had seen that first morning, but similar, just a smaller collection. A village, not a city?

"Rocks?" Maria said. "Or cooling towers? Termite mounds? Or fumarole cones? Giant white cacti? Anyone got any other suggestions? They're not in rows, but they do seem curiously regular, don't they?"

The careful silence was shattered by JC's booming laugh. "Houses? Huts? That's what we're all thinking, isn't it? A fine location by a river, good for hunting and fishing. Mid-latitude so the climate isn't too extreme. Sentients… Not high-tech, because there are no fields or boats. Also they haven't worked out yet that doors in the roof let the rain in. Maybe they need houses because they hibernate a third of the year. Maybe the trauma that killed the Galactic woman was a spear? Those huts are why

Duddridge chose that site. He never mentioned videos, but he didn't say the shuttle was too badly wrecked to maintain transmissions to the flotilla, now did he?"

"So why a yellow beacon, not purple, for sentience?" Hanna asked, her expression more skeptical than her voice.

Nothing was going to shake JC's jubilation. "Because of us, First, because of us! We shipped out before the end of the month. Galactic had ships in refit, but either they weren't quite ready, or the bosses wouldn't pay like I did for a preview of the data. We got away first, and when the monthly ISLA bulletin came out they knew *exactly* where we'd gone: a niner world! So they cut corners to get here first. They found this settlement on the river and started sending probes to investigate sentience, which GenRegs allow them to do. That didn't work, so they tried a shuttle. Finally they decided they needed heavier equipment to deal with the weather and went home to get it."

Everyone else was willing to leave the battle to Hanna.

"That still doesn't explain a yellow flag instead of a purple."

"Yes it does," JC insisted, "because if there are sentients, there are no profits. ISLA won't let you stake the world. There's fame and a billion-dollar bonus, but what are those to Galactic? Whoever the house builders are, without evidence of technology there's still room to argue whether or not they're truly sentient. Gorillas built nests, remember. Birds do. Duddridge probably wanted to consult the company higher-ups. He couldn't stake, but he certainly wanted to keep our fingers out of his pot. Yellow flag to scare us off."

"Stromatolites," Reese said airily.

JC glowered like a gorilla defending its nest. "What?"

"Stromatolites. I'm saying that your house builders are algae, or something similar. Stromatolites made some of the oldest fossils on Earth, but they still grow in a few places, especially in some highly saline tidal bays in Australia. They're stony mounds build by algae, like primitive reefs. Maria, is that a flood plain or an estuary?"

Maria consulted Control, which hedged and hawed, but eventually agreed with her that tides could come that far inland at some times of year and under certain weather conditions.

"Pretty damp houses, JC," Maria said. "But my guess is that the other shuttle went out to sea on the tide. The missing people may have done so, too. Control, show us some file pictures of stromatolites."

Stromatolites evidently came in groups of thousands on tidal flats, like swarms of stony beehives, all much the same height. The Cacafuego mounds seemed larger than terrestrial examples, but the similarity was close enough. Life never repeated itself exactly. On Shangri the tigers had six legs and spiders five. Without admitting defeat, JC subsided into a sulk.

"Why don't we call them 'chimneys' for now?" Jordan said with professional tact. "Until we know what they are. Any more questions or discussion?"

Seth said, "I'd like to ask Reese about chirality. But please dumb it down to my level."

"You're not dumb, Broderick," Reese said, "You're just crazy. Tell us what you know. That'll be quicker."

"I know that our bodies are mostly made of proteins, which are made up of chemicals called amino acids, and amino acids are asymmetric molecules. Like gloves."

"Top of the class. Life on Earth and almost all the thousands of life-bearing worlds we know of uses left-handed amino acids and right-handed sugars, but we're not certain why."

"Not just life," Maria said. "Amino acids in meteorites are biased also, just not so much. It starts with the magnetic fields around black holes."

Reese did not enjoy being interrupted. "That's still controversial. The only exceptions I know of are two exoplanets, Toyama and Verdant. Their amino acids are right-handed."

"And people died on Toyama from breathing the air?" Seth asked.

Reese frowned. "I don't know about breathing the air, but you certainly couldn't survive on a Verdant or Toyama diet. Your enzymes wouldn't fit the molecules, and some optical isomer pairs have very different properties. You'd starve if you weren't poisoned first."

"Poison is what I'm wondering about. According to the beacon's story, the Galactic prospectors died very suddenly. Could they have been poisoned by amino acids with the wrong handedness?"

There was silence while Reese cogitated. Control would refuse to speculate on such questions.

Eventually she said, "I don't see why isomer poisoning would be speedier than any other. If you go downside here you're going to be heading into the jaws of death anyway, with your life dependent on maintaining asepsis and avoiding all types of biohazards. Isomers aren't likely to be any more deadly than microbes or virus particles or allergens or heavy metals or poison gases or of the other things you studied in training. I suspect that radioactive dust may be a problem, because of Cacafuego's very high density, but you'll check on that. Optical isomerism is an interesting point, and I shall certainly check the samples for it when you provide some."

"Thanks," Seth said. "I hope to try."

Now he had the ball. Everyone was looking at him.

"Control tells me that you've put yourself on a course of anti-narcosis pills," Jordan prompted, looking grim.

"Yes, sir. Just a precautionary measure. The high partial pressure of nitrogen shouldn't be a problem in the short term." The long term would undoubtedly be fatal for all kinds of reasons.

"You've been having very mixed success with your simulated landings."

Of course the captain had been asking Control what Seth had been up to, and probably everyone else had too. But none of them had asked what parameters he had been changing. He knew that much because Control had told him so and, while Control might refuse to answer a question, it would never tell a lie.

"No eye-popping flash of genius," Seth said. "Just caution."

"Caution as in two-handed Russian roulette?" Reese said.

Seth ignored that. "The original mission plan called for two descents, with four or five touchdowns on each flight. We have to forget that, because the additional gravity we didn't expect will gobble up fuel on the ascent and those winds will eat even more. Even for a single touchdown, shuttle fuel will be a concern. Secondly, Control is starting to get a feel for the weather. I need it to forecast calm periods a few hours in advance with reasonable confidence, and in a day or so it should be able to do that. Then I make a fast descent, using power to shed orbital velocity fast. That takes up even more fuel, but gets me down before the weather patterns change.

"So fuel is a major problem. Two flights, with one touchdown apiece, are all we can reasonably hope for. Control's standard algorithm for a landing simulation presumes a minimum of one hour on the ground and takes weather into consideration when calculating the outcome. It turns out that landing is not the problem. The simulations I've run show that almost all landings are successful." He noted JC's smile. No one else seemed very convinced.

"The problem is the one-hour layover. Calms that long don't happen very often on Cacafuego. Wind gusts are unpredictable, even on fine days. *We have no way to tie our shuttle down.* We know what happened to *De Soto*'s, which is at least a three-seater. When I change Control's parameters to limit downtime to fifteen minutes, then the odds of a successful landing and takeoff are better than nine in ten."

"Fifteen minutes?" Jordan said. "You can't even exit the shuttle for the first ten minutes because its skin is too hot from the descent. You think you can disembark, plant a flag for the cameras, load a sample into the hopper, and get back aboard in five minutes? In 1.62 gees? That's ridiculous."

"Yes, sir. Any longer than that and my chances of survival drop very quickly." Seth answered the captain's question, but he was looking at JC. "I guess you're right. It just isn't worth it."

The look was the message, and the big man heard it like a fire-alarm; haggling over money was his business. He sprang to his feet, flushed and furious. "If you will allow us a five-minute adjournment, Captain, I need a private word with the prospector."

Seth rose also, holding a poker face, and followed in silence as the commodore stormed through the mess and galley until they reached the elevator. A ship's myth held that the elevator was the only place aboard not bugged by Control, so conversations there were private. Seth had never believed that, but if JC did, then it was probably true. JC, after all, had begun his career as an IT engineer. He would know Control inside and out.

The moment they were both inside and the door closed, Seth said, "Elevator to simulated Cacafuego gravity and make it snappy."

The elevator dropped rimwards, halting with a jolt that made even him gasp, while JC looked as if he just sustained a double hernia. His knees buckled and he had to grab the walls to save himself from falling.

"What the flaming shit did you do that for, boy?"

"We're at 1.62 gee, sir. A demonstration. Start by touching toes." He bent over and laid his palms on the floor. That had always been easy for him, and an extra fifty kilos on his shoulders make it easier than ever. Straightening up was more of a challenge.

Give him his due, JC did bend until his fingers were below his knees. He even managed to straighten again from there. "So?"

"So this is what you'd be sending me into, sir."

"It's what you're here for. I chose four people for brains and you for brawn. No fucking brains required."

"Brawn won't help me deal with hurricanes and Ebola fever."

"The day I hired you, boy, I warned you about the odds of surviving a first landing on a virgin world. But Galactic's team have paid that price, so you're on a second visit. Now we're forewarned, the odds should be better."

"Those odds, sir, are based on visits that all looked a lot safer than that before the sucker pressed the START button. This one looks like suicide already."

Veins showed in JC's forehead. "Sonny, I've been around a long time and I know how to read people. I am certain that Galactic found something that got Commodore Duddridge all fired up like a cat in a carwash. He gave up the hunt for the missing prospectors awful easy, didn't he?"

Seth agreed with a show of reluctance. "Yes sir. I did notice that."

"Weren't the landing team wearing monitors? He must have known exactly where they were, what their heart rate and blood pressure were. He didn't tell us they were dead, did he? He gave up on his own missing people and went after bigger game."

"Such as what?"

"I don't know yet. Big, obviously. Very big, because ISLA will eat his ass out for it when he gets home. They'll pull his license. He may face a civil suit for manslaughter. Galactic should fire him and cancel his bonus. So he's obviously gambling that it won't. He thinks he's found the treasure map, but he doesn't say what spot the X is marking. Now tell me how much more you want."

"More?"

"Don't play idiot. You just want more." JC took a menacing step closer, which would have been amusing even if his extra weight hadn't made him stagger.

Seth obligingly caught his arm to steady him. "Let's think about the same share as the captain, three percent?"

"Flaming shit, boy! You're dreaming in ten dimensions."

"I have one life only."

JC tried the long stare technique. He should have remembered that it didn't work on Seth Broderick. He was trapped by the unexpected 1.6 gravity. On any other expedition, the biologist or planetologist could take over the prospector's duties for at least the preliminary sampling mission. Here no one else but Seth, and possibly not even he, could function..

He pulled loose of Seth's grip. "For what? One dirt sample and a shitty picture? That's all you're offering?"

Seth shook his head. "Two hours, maybe three. I doubt I'll be able to stand upright any longer than that. As many samples and pictures as I can get in that time."

The commodore frowned. "You can deliver that?"

"Two hours or no deal."

"Two percent, total."

"No. Three or no go."

The commodore snarled. "You realize that you're asking for a bigger share than I'd get, because the extra would have to come out of my pocket?"

Seth shrugged, which felt like lifting a barbell. "Whose ass are we discussing here?" His knees ached already.

Another hard stare, not so long. "That's a firm offer? If we promise you a danger bonus of an extra two and half percent above contract, you volunteer to go downside to Cacafuego, waiving any and all claims against the company and its officers? And you will spend not less than two hours gathering samples and taking pictures?"

"Yes, sir."

"No matter what else we may learn in the next few days? This must be a one-time discussion. No racking the price higher later."

"It's a deal, sir. I swear I will voluntarily fly the shuttle down to land on Cacafuego, no matter what else we see down there."

"And return! This extra is not payable to your heirs and successors."

Mean bastard! Luckily Seth had no dependents or heirs to worry about. "Agreed. I must return alive to *Golden Hind* with the samples to qualify for the bonus."

JC said, "Control, record this agreement between Mighty Mite Ltd. and Prospector Broderick as an addendum to his contract, to be valid as soon as he and I attach our personal sigs."

—*Done, Commodore,* said Control's disembodied voice.

JC smiled a *gotcha* smile: the elevator was bugged like everywhere else.

Seth grinned and offered a hand. "Pleasure doing business with you, sir."

"A man after my own heart." JC accepted the shake.

And screamed.

Seth had been waiting fifteen months to repay that squeeze in La Paz, with a little interest, but he was pretty sure that in winning the handshake he had lost the battle. He'd been outwitted somehow. Just like Commodore Duddridge, JC had given up too easily.

⋙ ✳ ⋘

Still massaging his knuckles, JC led the way back into the control room and four expectant stares.

"Boy Wonder believes he has found an answer to the landing problem. In return for an agreed sum of danger money, he will attempt a trip downside, while releasing the corporation from any and all liability. Does that satisfy you, Captain?"

Jordan had lost his cherubic grin. "I'm tempted to certify him insane. Let's hear the plan, Broderick."

Seth leaned back and tried to look relaxed. He didn't feel it. He had just committed to the most dangerous thing he had ever contemplated, by far, and he was fizzing. Walking on another world was his lifelong dream, and he would probably have agreed to go if his odds of returning were one in a thousand.

"To start with, we deploy more of the ferrets in orbit, to act as passive relays, so we have complete over-the-horizon connection between ship and shuttle." Even a brief gap in communications could be fatal. He got a nod from Maria, whose babies the probes were.

"Then we choose some landing sites. I'd like to keep Galactic's Apple as primary choice, because shots of their smashed shuttle could be valuable if we ever meet them in court. It's a good site anyway. But we'd better have backups, in case Apple socks in on my way down. As I said, I start with a fast descent, while Control keeps a weather-eye open. After we choose, I'll make the final approach very slow. That will waste even more fuel, but a few extra minutes in the lower atmosphere — and with luck a rainstorm — will cool off the skin, so I won't have to wait for that to happen. I'll be wearing my K333 suit even on the descent. Two minutes after set-down I jump out, plant a flag where the cameras can see me, and throw a sample of dirt in the hopper."

"And then leave?" Jordan asked suspiciously.

JC was frowning.

"No," Seth said. "I pull out my overnight bag and Control brings the shuttle back up to the ship to refuel."

He had to wait for the protests to die down, but JC was smiling again.

"I forbid this as too dangerous," Jordan said, blue eyes icy.

70

"I don't think you can, Captain," JC said with venomous politeness. "A landing is written into the original contract. Prospector Broderick has assessed the risk and freely volunteered to perform this duty, while holding his employer and the ship's officers free of liability for the consequences. He will not endanger the ship, only himself. You cannot reasonably stop him."

"I forbid it!" Jordan had flushed.

Now JC did. "Letting your love life overrule your duty, Spears? First Officer Finn, what do you say?"

Hanna bit her lip, looked down at her hands, and said, "I think I agree with the commodore, Captain. A landing is in the contract. He agrees."

Silence. Jordan did not answer. After a moment, Seth resumed his presentation.

"I estimate about three hours' turnaround for the shuttle, depending on where the ship is relative to Apple. As soon as it's ready and the weather looks reasonable, Control brings it down and picks me up."

"Which may not be for a week!" Jordan said. "This is suicide."

"Why, sir? I said we had no way of staking down the shuttle, but I can stake *me* down if the wind gets obstreperous. On that open ground I can lie flat and wait out winds that would utterly trash the shuttle. There should be no flying chimney pots or tree branches out there on the flats. Or I can shelter in Galactic's shuttle, which has been there a couple of weeks now, and must be well lodged. The EVA suit will keep me aseptic, if not comfortable, for a full Earth day in any climate. Even if I can't remove my mask to eat, I can drink from my water bottles, and a few days without food won't kill me. I can handle the atmosphere, as long as I'm careful with decompression later. I'll have my blazer along to deal with predators, if any. What is such a big deal?"

Jordan shook his head in despair. "Don't you ever get *scared*, man?"

"Sometimes," Seth said.

As often as possible. Danger he loved. Every mind housed at least one dragon, and that was his.

DAYS 411-412

First-footers are the bravest of the brave. They are almost invariably young men, because most women have more sense. Those boys know that their chances of dying downside are worse than the odds on a battlefield, and that whatever wipes them will likely be something no one has ever met before, or even thought of. Yet still they go.

Fonatelles, op. cit.

During the next two days, Seth had to explain it over and over to everyone except JC, who just wanted a sample and a video of the flag being planted. After that, whatever Duddridge might think he had found, Galactic would have to deal with JC. Seth Broderick's survival was not important — and in fact would be detrimental to the financial bottom line. Remembering how easily the commodore had given in and granted him that extra two-and-a-half percent, Seth wondered if he might have signed his own death warrant.

The others came at him in groups or one at a time. Seth couldn't see why everyone else was so excited. He even failed to get his point across to Jordan that evening. The captain dragged him into his cabin and produced a bottle of high quality whiskey, potent stuff. Then he tried his damnedest to talk Seth out of going downside at all.

"But this was always the plan," Seth said. "I'm the prospector, this is my job. Yes, Galactic screwed up. Two women and a man lost, that's tough. But we can learn from their mistakes. JC is right when he says Cacafuego needs heavier, tougher shuttles. If I can send back a sample with any pharmaceutical promise at all, Mighty Mite will find the money to build them."

Jordan was more cynical. "JC just wants to score off Galactic. He'll be all over the media. The multinational run away, but the great JC Lecanard and his little Mighty Mite start-up company persisted. They tamed the killer planet. Triumph of a lifetime."

"Jordie!" Seth said. That was the name he used when they were in bed together, it came close to insubordination when they were officer and crewmember. "I'm not doing it for JC. I'm doing it for me."

"You won't get a mention."

"I don't want a mention. I want to be choke-on-it rich. Apart from that, I'm my own audience."

"You'll be your own chief mourner, too." The captain refilled the glasses with a generous hand.

"Stuff it! I thrive on adrenalin with a side order of testosterone. Gives me a hard-on, so I go for it, whatever it is."

"Reese is right. You're crazy."

"Sorry, buddy," Seth said. "I don't mean to worry you." Being worried about was a very strange experience. Unique. "I'll be all right."

"I hope so. I really hope so. I'd miss you."

Seth drained his glass just to give himself a coughing fit. It didn't help. As soon as he got his breath back he found that he had to go on. "Nobody's ever ... I'm not used to ... I don't know how to say this. I know ISLA tested us for claustrophobia and we all rated zero, but I am heartily sick of living in this pill box."

"We all are."

"So I dream of all the things I'm going to do when we get home. Even if all we walk away with is two years' back pay, I feel like I'm going to blow it all and then go back to being a bouncer, if that's all I can find. Bungee jumping, mountain climbing, scuba caving ... the wilder the better ... Lordie, Jordie, in my dreams you're always there with me. I guess what I'm trying to say is, you're special. Never met anyone... Oh, balls! Now I'm drowning in clichés. I don't care what anatomy you're sporting, you're the best company I ever known. I get along better with you than anyone else I've ever met. I know this will sound absurd in this time and place, but if we both get home alive and rich, then I'll ask you to marry me." It sounded so odd, he said, "That's the truth, Jordie. Mean it."

Jordan did not look startled, so he must have foreseen this madness. He shook his head sadly.

"Shipboard romances never wear well."

"This one will, I promise."

"No one I'd rather shack up than you, Seth. For a while, certainly. Years, maybe, but marriage won't work. Once in a while a herm and a woman make it, but herm and man never. Men resent being cut off every second month. And sooner or later they want kids. We're sterile. You know that."

"So we'll adopt. I am one hundred percent serious. Marry me!"

Jordan shook himself, or perhaps just shivered violently. "Go and first-foot Cacafuego, Seth. Come back safely, please, please come back safely! Bring the Holy Grail back with you and anything you want in the galaxy will be yours."

"Including you?"

"If that's your choice."

Seth said, "Good." Then he changed the subject. He could discuss anything with the female Jordan, but man-to-man sentiment made him uncomfortable.

⁕

Hanna cornered him in the mess when he'd just sat down to eat breakfast. Her red hair blazed like a warning beacon.

"We have only one shuttle."

He wanted to say that he'd already noticed that, but his mouth was full of cherry Danish, so he just nodded.

"One landing may be a justifiable risk, but two is tempting fate. If it crashes the second time, you'll be stranded down there forever."

Or the first time, ditto. He swallowed and tried yet again to explain that a single grab sample would be very unlikely to provide reliable data on the planet's pharmaceutical potential. A dozen varied samples gathered over a visit of several hours would be a million times more valuable. He didn't mention that Control had now confirmed seeing a storm surge reach as far inland as the Apple site. The good news was the sea would have brought in samples for him to pick up. The bad news was that next time it might collect him for its own use.

Hanna was as stubborn as a squeaky floorboard, but she could recognize when she had met her match. "Why are you doing this, Seth?"

"For money."

"Money to do what, Seth? Buy women? Big houses? You think those will make you happy?"

"Haven't thought about happy," he admitted. Happiness was doing crazy things, so he was happier now than he had ever been. "I'm doing this because I signed a contract. I gave my word. It looks dangerous, yes, but it's doable and while I don't go to church every week, I do regard my word as sacred."

"You squeezed more money out of JC."

"Yes, but if he'd balked and called me on it, I'd have gone down anyway." He wondered if that might even be true.

"What comes after, Seth?"

"More of the same? You come with me on my next jaunt?"

The Big Nothing was notoriously addictive. Few wildcatters ever readjusted to life downside when they got back. Even those who struck it rich on their first voyage often went back out again to hunt for bigger dreams, for El Dorado or the Fountain of Youth, the jackpot beyond the rainbow. He could, of course, ask Hanna why she was back in space, having made a small fortune on her first trip out. He didn't. Nor did he explain to her that danger gave him a thrill in his groin.

Hanna sighed. She was a very pretty woman.

"I shall pray for you, Seth."

"Don't you always?"

She bristled. "Pray for your safe return, I mean. I always pray that you will see the error of your lecherous ways."

Lecherous? He? Seth Broderick? He was behaving like any healthy male animal would in the presence of mature mating partners. He was tempted to suggest she go and exchange notes with Reese about sexual peculiarities.

→═◎ 🗡 ◎═←

Golden Hind orbited Cacafuego in less than an hour. It rarely passed directly over Sombrero, but the unmanned probes' limited sensing ability contributed some data. Control was gradually building up a picture of tide and weather patterns.

As the forecasts became less erratic — they would never be truly reliable — Seth kept perfecting his plans. He could hope for a minimum stay downside of three hours, but he must allow for eight or nine as more likely. That was half a day for Cacafuego's nineteen-hour rotation. If the weather turned nasty all bets were off, but he would die of thirst or infection before he starved. His

K333 suit would protect him from heat stroke, and the climate was not as extreme at that latitude as it was at the poles.

The main reason for choosing Apple, of course, was that Galactic had chosen it, and their fleet would have had more advanced remote scanning equipment than *Golden Hind* did. Apple had one of the cryptic "villages" and Maria was offering fifty-fifty odds that there was a pool of open water beside the wrecked shuttle. Pools were always promising collection sites.

The team conferred and chose alternative target sites: Banana, Cherry, and Damson, all selected more because they lay along an extension of the likely flight path to Apple, than because they seemed any better. Cherry offered another of the strange "villages". Banana and Damson lay in the lea of mountain ranges, which might provide some shelter from storms.

Seth spent hours in the prospector's storeroom, deciding what he must take with him, adding and subtracting gadgets and equipment. Nobody bothered him there, but the choices did. How many spare breathing filters? He must take a stun gun in case he saw some small fauna that he could capture. Was taking the blazer as well worth the extra weight? In the end he decided to leave out the blazer. *Golden Hind*'s telescope should detect any animal life larger than a small pony and had not done so. A stun gun would stop anything smaller than that. How much drinking water? How many samples would he be able to carry?

→═◎ ✕ ◎═←

Maria cornered him in the showers that evening while he was cleaning his teeth.

"Seth? Lover boy?"

He cocked an eyebrow at her image in the mirror, admiring the way her nipples stretching the thin fabric. She idled fingers down his bare back.

"Apart from JC," she said, "everyone aboard is totally opposed to what you're planning: Jordan, Hanna, Reese, and me."

"Whittington's cool. I promised you'll feed her double while I'm gone."

"Is there anything we can offer to make you change your mind?" She was wearing a come-on expression, but Maria always wore a come-on expression. She honestly didn't know that, and never understand why men pestered her so much.

"Nothing. Not a trillion dollars." What in space would impress Maria? "Even you can't offer me what Cacafuego offers — fame, immortality! There will be species named after me, chemicals, minerals. And my humble contribution may lead to great scientific discoveries!"

She did not seem impressed. Her fingers slid around to his abs. "You're such a great stud, Seth, the most exciting man I've ever—"

She was interrupted by an announcement from Control.

—Prospector, as requested, this is a four-hour forecast of a window of calm conditions at Site Apple. Launch window is open for next twenty-two minutes.

Seth's heart leaped. His groin thrilled. He forgot Maria; this was better.

"Control, start loading shuttle fuel. Excuse me, love. That's my cue."

✶

He was still pulling on his top when he reached the mess. Everyone else was there, having been playing a four-handed game of 3-D backgammon. Obviously they had heard the forecast, or else they had primed Control to warn them when it warned him, because they all tried to crowd around and speak at once.

"Sorry, can't stay! Business." He plowed through them, heading for the elevator. He was stopped at the galley door by JC's mighty bellow:

"Prospector!"

"Sir?"

"It is traditional that the master names the shuttle."

Recalling Reese's sneer about barrels, Seth said, *"Niagara."* He stepped through the door and was gone.

✶

Launching a shuttle ought to be a deliberate, meticulous procedure. In this case he and Control had already done everything that could be done in advance. By the time he scrambled into his chair, Control was showing the remaining items of the checklists on the display and proceeded to read them out as they were completed or reached significant marks.

—Fuel loading, sixty percent complete.

—All hatches secured.

—Sixteen minutes left in launch window.

—Battery power ok.

—Fuel loading, seventy percent complete.

—External radiation acceptable.
—Fuel loading, eighty percent complete.
—Ten minutes left in launch window.
—Revised weather forecast: unacceptable.

That was a punch he had not seen coming. For a moment he was tongue-tied. When he found words, they came out in a croak. "What'ja mean 'unacceptable?'"

—Torrential rain and winds above shuttle specifications are now predicted for Site Apple at estimated time of touchdown.

"How much above spec?"

—Double.

If that were a human voice, he would think it was mocking him.

"Abort launch. Unload fuel." He was dismayed to realize that he was soaked in sweat and his heart was racing around his chest, beating on his ribs as if trying to escape. Shame on him!

"Tough one," Jordan's voice said from the screen. "But the stars will line up again soon."

⇥ ✷ ⇤

About four hours into *Day 412*, the stars did line up and Seth had to start over, running along the corridor before he was properly awake. That time the launch was aborted even before he reached the cab. He went back to bed happily, knowing that he would have a few hours' respite now, while *Golden Hind*'s orbit took it out of shuttle range of Site Apple. When he awoke, the downside weather was worse than ever. Close to noon he was called again and had to abort at T minus three minutes — another hurricane winding up.

Jordan called a conference that evening.

Seth saw no smug faces around the table. They were all feeling the strain, but they all seemed sympathetic, even JC. No one suggested he give up. They knew he wouldn't.

"You can't keep on like this," Jordan said. "I know you've got titanium nerves and antifreeze blood, but no one can take this kind of jacking around for long without losing their edge. You've got to have some down-time. Ten hours off every night, at least."

He nodded. It made sense. The planet wouldn't go away. "I'll make that change tomorrow, if I'm still here. I'm not starting to crack yet." He forced a grin. "But I am *really* getting pissed off!"

Maria said, "We've checked Control's weather records, and there truly are no patterns, as the Galactic commodore said. The Coriolis forces are huge and the temperature gradients enormous.

Control's invented the Category Seven hurricane, and tracked three of them."

Hanna took over. "The problem is that the weather cannot be predicted more than three hours in advance, at best, which isn't long enough for your needs. Another strategy would be to launch to an unstable orbit that would take you down slowly, over two or three days. From there you could make a faster approach when the weather looked good."

But if he missed out on all four targets, he'd have to use fuel to boost his orbit, which in turn meant he would have to return to *Golden Hind* to refuel, and *Hind* didn't carry enough spare for him to start over. So then he'd be limited to the one-shot plan that he'd rejected earlier. His danger bonus would pop like a soap bubble.

"I don't like it," Jordan said. "He'd be sitting by himself in that barrel. Here at least he has company. He can eat properly and exercise. There's no hurry. We can stay here for months if we have to."

Seth was saved from having to decide right then by Control.

—*Prospector, as requested, this is a four-hour forecast of...*

Seth emptied his water glass and stood up. "Control, start loading shuttle fuel." This time he would walk, not run. "Gotta go, friends."

"Good luck!" Jordan called.

"We're praying for you." That was Hanna, of course.

"We're betting on you." That was JC.

⊷⊷◉ ✳ ◉⊷⊷

He scrambled into the cab.

—*Fuel loading, seventy percent complete.*

—*All hatches secured...*

He knew it all by heart now; he could sing along if he wanted to. He tried not to watch the fuel gauge. Cacafuego was just rising over the edge of the ship's disk, blue and white and patches of green. Very beautiful; very deadly. He hunted for Sombrero Island among the white loops and whirls. He was taken by surprise when a tone sounded and the screen flashed green text: *Ready to launch.*

Gulp.

"*Niagara* to *Golden Hind*. Request clearance to launch."

"You are cleared to launch, Master." Jordan.

"Bring me back a diamond." That was Reese, with a joke that must be older than she was.

The *START* button lit up. Seth pushed it and was on his way.

Niagara rose gently and almost silently, just a slight vibration. Once clear of the ship, it turned to shed orbital velocity. He watched the edge of the disk go by, then the greater mass behind it, in the part they called the tower, the tokamak generators. He watched for signs of damage, but saw none and had not expected to.

In a few minutes he had left the ship behind and was floating over the planetscape of Cacafuego. He felt almost drunk with joy. He had achieved his life's ambition, to go exploring in the Big Nothing. He could even cling to the illusion that he was alone, although the back of his mind knew that five people were watching his progress very carefully. He hoped — for their sakes almost more than his own — that they wouldn't have to abandon him the way Commodore Madison Duddridge had deserted his people.

JC's voice: "Commodore to Master. Don't forget to plog. Gotta keep the kiddies happy. Commodore out."

Seth muttered an obscenity. A plog was a prospector's log, and a valuable part of the expedition record. The contract required him to record a commentary during EVA, and he ought to start now. Traditionally, the rights to the plog belonged to the person who made it, and there were many sly rumors of prospectors who had made more money out of their plogs than their employers had made out of the voyages.

He talked for a while about the view, his lifelong ambition to be a prospector, and the dangers of bad weather. He mentioned that Galactic had lost prospectors but was careful not to hint that they had been marooned. Then he signed off to prepare for landing. He fetched his EVA suit and left it handy. He put his two bags by the rear hatch, where he could kick them out.

"Control, report weather forecast for Site Apple."

—*Calm at estimated touchdown and for one hour thereafter.*

"It seems that the weather window is narrowing," he told his plog. "The ship's computers cannot predict this planet's weather more than an hour or two ahead. A strong gale would wreck this shuttle once it's on the ground, and a Category One hurricane is a mild breeze by local standards. I need a clear two hours' sampling. As soon as I land, therefore, I will send *Niagara* back to the mother ship to refuel…"

He was a private, self-contained person and hated this mindless, anonymous chatter.

→═◎　✳　◎═←

He was eating a sandwich, which might be his last meal for a long time, when Control announced go-no-go point for an Apple descent. The decision was his, but out of courtesy he called home.

"*Niagara* to *Golden Hind*. You see any problems?"

Jordan's face appeared in the viewer. "Negative. All looks clear to us for a landing and prompt take-off. Good luck, Master."

"Thanks. Start synthesizing a roast ox for the banquet tomorrow. *Niagara* out. Control, landing confirmed. Use cold-skin approach."

The cold-skin approach would waste more fuel, exuding it from pores in the hull to cool it, but he had fuel to spare now that he was committed to the first choice landing site, and the faster his exit from the shuttle, the less time it must sit on the ground and be vulnerable.

A short burst of the rockets began the final descent into the atmosphere. He stripped and put on the EVA suit. It was a marvel of technology and plumbing, light and comfortable, yet strong enough to stop a shark's bite, airtight, air-conditioned, and able to change color when needed. Cameras on the helmet would send a visual record of anything he looked at back to *Golden Hind*. His heartbeat and other personal statistics would also be reported. He attached a scoop, knife, water bottle, sample wipes, and the stun gun. By the time he had checked all the circuits and gadgets, Control was warning him to strap in for turbulence. The shuttle had begun final approach, angling down over a blue enamel sea.

"I hope you can make out those whitecaps, and there are some shapes over to starboard that look to be whale-sized. Whether they're mammals or reptiles or jellyfish we don't know, and they may be some other type never met anywhere else." They might just be seaweed, but seaweed wasn't romantic. "Those misty peaks are the southern coastal range of Sombrero Island, which is our destination. We are approaching from the west, aiming for the site named Apple, on the eastern coast. I am really feeling the gravity now."

Deceleration, in fact, but he could edit that out of the published version.

He explained how the fog on the wings was fuel being exuded to cool the ship so that he could make a quick exit when it landed.

He did not comment on the stall light flickering orange as Control spun out the approach as long as possible.

"A very rocky coast in sight now. Just look at those breakers! Big waves do not necessarily mean strong winds near here, of course. The storm may be a long way away. The swell outruns the wind, and this is a planet-sized ocean. You may think that looks like great surfing, but low-gravity planets offer better. Waves ten stories high were sighted on Pixie."

The interior plains of Sombrero were green, with meandering rivers, but he was too high to see any detail. The central peaks looked volcanic, but he decided not to say so. He could ask Maria later.

"The eastern sea is just coming into view ahead." So was a major storm to the south, cloud tops dazzlingly white, ominous lightning flashes underneath. "I'm turning up the magnification on this screen to take a look at that cluster of what we're calling chimney rocks over there. These are a major mystery, one of the things I have to check out. We don't know what they are or what makes them.

"*Niagara*'s coming in about treetop height, except there are no trees, at least not here. Less than fifty meters. The plain is very green, but not grass. You can see it waving in the wind gusts."

The cabin display was showing wind gusting to sixty klicks. Control wouldn't try landing in that. Damn! Damn! Damn! Keep hoping.

"The sandy channels are the distributaries in the delta of a great river, mostly dry now because it's summertime and we're too far from the equator for glaciers. There's a bigger arm over there; lots of water in that one; this place gets a lot of rain." He would edit out all this rubbishy babble. "And that white thing straight ahead in that smaller channel is the wreck of one of Galactic's shuttles. I am planning to land close to that because... Here we go!"

Niagara tilted to the vertical, jets flashed fire, and ... and hovered, drifting.

"It looks like I'm not going to be able to..."

What? Why? The wind gauge had dropped to twenty klicks, just a gentle breeze hereabouts, but the shuttle was floating over the greenery, moving steadily farther away from the wreck.

—*Looking for level ground, Prospector.*

It all looked level to him, but Control had radar. The vegetation was thrashing in the wash from the jets, as well as in the wind. This hovering ate fuel at a murderous rate. His chatter dried up as he stared in horror at the fuel gauge. Forty-six … forty-five … Forty-one was the point of no return. When the numbers showed that, Control would blast back into orbit… Forty-three…

The shuttle gently settled down in a roiling mass of smoke.

Then came silence — and sheer panic as the shuttle began to tilt. He added some comments that would certainly have to be cut. If the undercarriage could not find a level footing, the engines would fire again and the landing would be aborted.

That almost happened but didn't. He started breathing again when *Niagara* came to rest at a Tower of Pisa slant. Even that could be a fatal problem. The ground might be rocky and uneven, but soft goo was far more likely in a flat area with high rainfall. Mud had been known to trap shuttles permanently. Blackadder's Law: *Every world is different, except they're all out to get you.* Which way was the wind blowing? Even a middling gust from the wrong direction would tip him over. *Move!*

He unbuckled his harness. "*Niagara* has landed — a little off vertical, but it seems to be stable. I see the wind is clocked at a bracing twenty-five klicks, probably the closest to dead calm we ever get around here. Temperature is forty-one Celsius, humidity ninety-two. My EVA suit will keep me comfortable. I am now starting down the shaft we call the Gut. You will see how Control closes the bulkhead hatches above me as I pass each one. That's to prevent contamination of the ship when I open the outer hatch. I am really conscious of the high gravity. At my weight it makes me tote an extra sixty kilos or so and I notice it just holding the rungs of the ladder.

"Now I'm at the door, but Control will not open it until the outer skin is cool enough to touch. I expect to find smoke outside there. The landing jets will have fired the vegetation, but my suit is fireproof and my helmet filters the air I breathe. Even the two packs at my feet are fireproof. Ah!"

The clock in his helmet display tipped over to *Day 413*.

The door fell open.

Outside he saw the triangular shadow of the shuttle, like a giant arrow pointing the way to fortune for Seth Broderick. The nearby vegetation was charred, but it must be too wet to burn well. White smoke was streaming away in the wind, staying close to the ground. He kicked out his packs, noting how they fell as if shot out of a cannon; then he turned and gingerly clambered down the ladder on the inside of the door. Because of the shuttle's tilt, the last rung was about a meter above the ground. Normally he would have jumped, but the packs made the landing tricky and a twisted ankle could kill him now. He lowered himself by his arms, which was not the easiest thing he had ever done.

Golden Hind opened the circuit just long enough for him to hear them all cheering, but he was too busy looking around at the world to respond.

DAY 413

The public and the wildcatters themselves glamorize the first-footers. They're an all-right gang, of course, but I've always been more impressed by the second wave, the ones who go down to gather up the first ones' bones.

Fonatelles, op. cit.

⇥⊸ ✦ ⊸⇤

He had expected something like grassland — not a putting green, of course, but a tussocky meadow. He should have known better. What Cacafuego had laid out as a welcome mat was a boulder field, giant shingle on a chaotic scale, with everything from gravel up to rocks as big as bathtubs. For three meters out from the shuttle the rocks had been blackened by the landing jets, but beyond that the ground was hidden under a dense mat of ropy roots or vines, from which sprouted ferny green stuff about waist high.

Of the shuttle's five legs, one was contracted as far as it would go, two were fully extended, and one of those did not even reach the ground. The result looked highly unstable. If the wind veered about thirty degrees to the east, Control would very likely slam the door shut and lift off. It lacked enough fuel to hunt for a better site nearby. His EVA suit was fireproof but it could not save him from being boiled alive. He didn't mention all that to his plog. It could be dubbed in later, if there was a later.

He hoisted one of the packs and carried it out of range, then came back for the other. They were heavy but the footing was horrible, even when he could see where he was stepping. He tore off a couple of fronds, wound them into a wad, and rolled them in a sample wipe — which looked like an ordinary sheet of sandwich wrap, but at once sealed itself and evacuated the air. Loamy soil and scummy water were the two best sites to find potentially pharmaceutical materials, but neither was handy. He tried tearing up one of the creeper vines, but could not budge it.

Then his eye was caught by a tiny movement. He was being watched. In shape it was most like a terrestrial lizard, about as long as his hand. In color it was trying to match the half-blackened rock on which it sat, but not succeeding very well. Fire would be rare on this rain-sodden island. Seth slowly drew his stun gun, set it to low, and froze the little critter. He picked it up.

"Sorry, wee fellow. Hey, you've got six legs! Aren't you lucky?"

And so was he. Plants were just sunlight-eaters, sugar-makers, and much less diverse than fauna. There could be no argument with a new animal species. Chemists would drool over this evidence. He wrapped it in a wipe and dropped it in his collecting pocket.

"Captain to Master. Your fifteen minute planned stay is almost up. Our view of your location is through a probe, not direct. We don't see any major storms lurking, but don't rely on that too much."

Especially when the shuttle was balanced on a hair.

"Copied and out." Seth trudged back to the open door and threw the two samples inside. "Control, close door."

Then he had to retrace his steps to the packs and squat to take out the flag. His knees were weary already. The flagpole was telescopic, but where could he plant it? It would be very unimpressive peeking over the shrubbery. He tried a patch of finer gravel, but the shaft went in only a few centimeters, not enough. He jammed it between two of the burned boulders, then turned to face *Niagara*.

"Can you see me clearly?"

"You're beautiful!" That was JC, excited. "Wave for all your teeny plog fans. Now get farther back and send *Niagara* home."

Easier said than done. The vegetation completely hid the ground, and kept writhing in the wind. While the boulders underneath seemed fairly stable, being locked in place by the creeper, he had to feel for every foothold. If he tangled a foot and tripped, he would very likely twist or break something. After about ten meters he turned.

"Control, return to mother ship for refueling."

—Crewmember still ashore. Confirm instructions.
Does it think he was not aware of that? "Departure confirmed."

White flames and smoke burst out around the shuttle's under-carriage. *Niagara* soared up on pillars of fire and turned to the east. No birds flew up in alarm. The sky was a clear blue, but uncluttered by circling vultures. Evolution did not favor wings on high-gee worlds.

A stray buffet of wind blew the flag over.

⟶⬤ ✴ ⬤⟵

Seth Broderick had a planet all to himself. He was as alone as a guy ever could be. Frustratingly, all he could see of his world was groundcover and a charred area like the scar of a large campfire. Control had avoided ridges when choosing a stable landing ground, so he was standing in a very slight hollow. He plodded up the gentle slope, arms spread to keep his balance, placing every step with care. Top speed was half a klick an hour now. He chattered to his plog.

"If you've watched many plogs, then I'm sure you've heard other prospectors say this, but I really wonder what this world smells like. The filter on my suit cuts out all the odors and dust..." He paused to catch his breath. "Another strange thing here is the silence. This is a very silent place. No birds singing, no dogs or traffic... Just the wind swishing this groundcover."

At the top of the slope he found the chaotic rocks and pebbles more exposed, as if this were a later dump from some great fleet of trucks. Here the vegetation had not been burned, but he found dead remains of the ropy vines under some of the boulders, and collected a few fragments.

Although he was still standing on a plain, he had gained a slightly wider view. The sun was low in the sky, roughly north-north-east, but it would not set at this latitude yet, so he need not worry about darkness. The Tsukuba River lay somewhere to the north, heading eastward to the sea. Southeastward stood an ominous wall of cloud, not the storm he had flown over, another just as menacing. The chimneys must lie in that direction. To the south he ought to be able to discern the coastal ranges, but all he was sure of were some clouds that might be the sort that hung around above mountains.

To the north he thought he could see a white triangular wing pointed skyward, the remains of the Galactic shuttle, perhaps half a kilometer away. He had planned on being set down much closer to it.

"*Golden Hind,* can you place me?"

Jordan: "Your landing site was about 1.2 kilometers west of the chimneys. The Galactic shuttle is 0.6 klicks northeast of you."

Right on! "And the river?"

"The major channel is at least three klicks north of the shuttle, but remember there are many minor channels."

"Then I shall investigate the shuttle first and after that proceed to the colony. I doubt if I'll get any farther over this terrain. What is Maria making of it? I was expecting alluvium — mud, not boulders. Is this crap glacial?"

"Maybe originally glacial," Maria said. "The nearest I've ever seen are debris flows that you get in major floods. But that's in mountains; I've never heard of anything quite like it on a river plain. Some of the rocks look well-rounded and some are freshly broken. It's very poorly sorted — big stuff jumbled in with much finer. I can't be sure without a closer look, but I suspect you're seeing the product of those storm surges Control predicted. The river probably floods, but I can't believe any river could throw boulders of that size around on what is basically flat ground. Anything that can do so must be extremely violent."

"I can't wait to meet it. Thanks. Prospector out."

He made his way back down to his packs and collected two spare water bottles. He could always locate the packs by their transponders, but he very much doubted that he would be coming back for them.

⊷⊶ ✳ ⊷⊶

Wading over that rubble in that gravity felt much like climbing a mountain while carrying a horse. It took him well over an hour to reach the shuttle, a distance he could have run in two minutes on Earth. Several times he nearly fell. Level patches were bad enough; the gentlest slopes, up or down, were even harder, because terrestrial eyes and reflexes couldn't judge what was needed.

Still the only sound was the rush of the wind in the shrubbery. Every ten or fifteen minutes he heard that sound rising and lay down until it stopped howling and the wind dropped to a strong breeze again. Twice he thought he was going to be lifted bodily, and certainly would have been had he not had the vegetation to hang on to. He understood now how Dylan Guinizelli had let a gust of wind break his arm.

He collected a thumb-sized, four-legged beetle, a few stray weeds unlike the ferns, some fibrous material that he guessed was decayed wood-like matter left there by the storm surges, three broken shells with traces of organic material clinging to them, some tiny animal bones, and a dozen fecal pellets. Those would probably excite Reese more than all the rest. A single gram of organic material would yield thousands of exotic chemicals, but he found it hard to believe his packet of grunge would ever make him rich, despite the legends of old Mathewson and his bucket of dirt. It was not an inspiring collection and he might have to return with his sample bag more empty than full — unless, of course, he found some of the Galactic samples he could purloin. There would be a certain justice in that.

He had used up at least a third of his planned stay. He was tired. He was thirsty, and had emptied his first water bottle. Why couldn't the damned planet have given him a nice flat meadow to run around on, as he had expected? A delta plain made of boulders was an absurdity.

Long before he reached the Galactic shuttle, he saw that it was a KR745, which could carry a team of five and made *Golden Hind*'s Oryo 9 look like a child's toy. It had probably cost twenty times as much. JC liked to badmouth the multinationals, but even he never accused them of skimping on equipment. Seth found where the KR745 had touched down, charring the vegetation. He found the scars where it had dragged and bounced as the wind took it away. And he came at last to the gully where it now rested.

The KR745 had the standard delta wings for supersonic flight, but it was a "layflat" as opposed to a "standup" like *Niagara*. It landed level, not vertical. That might have been its undoing, if the crew had not appreciated the wind danger soon enough. Control should have done so, but with the two prospectors gone exploring, the biologist left aboard must have overruled Control's advice to take off. Now what had once been a beautiful thing was an ugly corpse, lying like a dead bird in a shallow, sandy channel, resting on its port side against the far bank, with one wing pointing at the sky and the other crumpled underneath the fuselage. Its back had been broken, leaving the nose almost separated from the rest.

The channel was sinuous, its bed sandy not rocky, the first fine-grained sediment Seth had seen. No water was flowing, but Maria had been right about open water near the wreck, a shiny pond, rippling in the wind. More pools marking the low points of the channel, even on the limited stretch he could see before it curved out of view. Would they be salt tidal pools, or seepages of fresh groundwater from the river? He had no intention of tasting them to find out, but he would certainly take samples.

He was babbling about this to his plog when Jordan's voice interrupted.

"Prospector, the shuttle will dock in about ten minutes. We can begin refueling at once, but how does the weather look down there?"

Weather? Seth glanced eastward and then used some words that would certainly have to be edited out before his plog could ever be made public. The storm was halfway up the sky, white on the crest, but black as death underneath, lurid with lightning flashes.

"Not good," he added for publication. "What's the timing?"

"Not good either. We think that brute is going to hit you in about two hours, and *Niagara* can't get to you before then."

"Two hours should give me long enough to take a look at the chimneys. This wreck must have been lodged here for two or three weeks. I can shelter inside it until the wind drops."

"Keep in touch, Seth."

"Stick around, won't you? Prospector out."

The rocky bank sloped gently, but gentle in that gravity felt like steep elsewhere. He slid and staggered down it without falling. Then, at last free to step out normally, he headed along the hollow to the wreck. His objective was the gaping hole just forward of the wings, which looked like an easy access. He hadn't gone far when he saw the footprints, and those changed everything.

There were many prints, most of them old and faint, flattened by wind and rain until they were mere dimples in the sand. He might not have noticed them had they not been grouped into two distinct trails and highlighted by a few more recent tracks. Both trails began at the break in the shuttle. The wind had not yet had time to blur the latest set, although they did not look very recent. They were human footprints and their maker had been barefoot — reasonable in this climate, dangerous in this environment. One set ran eastward to the pond and the other west to a place where someone had been digging in the sand. Even your average Ph.D. could work out that the pond was for either drinking water or washing, while the digging site was a makeshift latrine. Animals dug pits, but not with a shovel.

Seth babbled to his plog about Man Friday and Robinson Crusoe while the rest of his brain raged against the extent of Commodore Duddridge's treachery. Some of his shuttle crew had survived until very recently. They might even be still alive. The commodore had not merely given up too easily, he had deliberately flown away and marooned people to die on a planet one step up from Hell. Then the bastard had tried to cover up his crime by posting a quarantine beacon in the hope that Mighty Mite's expedition would not come looking at the evidence. There was a charge of willful murder in Comrade Duddridge's future.

Seth's second thought — followed instantly by a surge of shame that he would think of such a thing at a time like this, when he had just discovered a fellow human being callously left to die — was that his financial future was now secure. If he returned alive to the real world, his plog was going to be a bestseller. It had all the syrupy drama and pathos of afternoon space opera, the sort of dreck churned out by teams of worn-out hacks to enliven the existence of Earth's hopeless millions. He would be famous.

Jordan's voice: "Are those prints human, Seth?"

"Yes, sir. Wait a minute, though…"

Seth laboriously lowered himself to his knees, and then crouched to view the sand at a low angle. The oblique sunlight helped. "The topmost set, yes," he said. "And some of the older ones. But there are other tracks mixed in, bigger feet. Can you see this one?" He traced it out for the camera's benefit: four toes in front, probably two behind. Or the other way around, of course. Every toe ended in a wicked claw. "Whatever it is, I don't think it eats grass."

He struggled to his feet again. "Now to look inside."

"Watch you don't get shot at," Jordan said.

Wise advice. Seth decided he was already close enough to open negotiations.

"Ship ahoy!" He shouted as loud as he could, knowing how his mask would muffle his voice. "Hello, Galactic! Anyone home? Anyone looking for a ride back to Earth?"

Nothing happened except that the sun went out. The storm had now spread from horizon to horizon, but the wind had dropped, for the first time since he arrived on Cacafuego. The ferns were barely moving. He walked closer to the shuttle.

There was a dead fish lying outside the opening.

This time his voice definitely quavered.

"Now that fish is odd. The position looks too deliberate to be just chance. There are no other dead fish anywhere, not that I can see. Is this one meant to be bait, placed there to lure some animal closer? Or has someone left an offering to the gods who live inside? Any new planet is interesting, but this one is starting to look bizarre." Also scary, even for him.

He shouted again. Still no response.

"I'm going closer."

The opening in the fuselage marked where the shuttle had almost broken in two, a great wound like the mouth of a cave. The entrance was low enough that he had to stoop to see in.

He clattered his stun gun against the side and turned on his helmet light to scan the shadowed interior. He was looking through the former underbelly into a shambles that had been the biosafety laboratory, now lying on its side. Much sand had washed in, largely burying the heaps of smashed equipment and furniture on what had been a wall and was now the floor. The sand had retained many footprints, some human, others … not. About human length, but broader and *webbed*. Giant penguins?

There were bones mixed in with the debris. Although they looked more like fish bones than human, they suggested that this might be something's lair. What something other than humans used a spade — which he now saw standing upright in the sand just inside?

There was a table, too, that had either landed almost exactly right way up or been placed in that position later. A drawer from a desk or chest stood upright on the table, handle at the top. Drawers in spacecraft did not fall out by accident, no matter how rough the turbulence, and he knew of no way that this one could have ended in that position unless it had been placed there by a sentient being.

The only exit from the lab had been in the forward bulkhead, now turned sideways so that the door hung open. He shouted again, and this time he heard a faint noise, more a groan than a cry. *And tapping!*

"I'm coming in!" An obstacle course in 1.6 gees with an unknown carnivorous species at the end of it was every boy's dream. Stun gun in hand, he ducked inside. A workbench against the former forward bulkhead was now turned sideways with its cupboard doors open. It made a practical ladder leading up to the door, but would it hold his now enormous weight?

"I'm coming!" he repeated.

More tapping, faster this time.

He clambered up to the door without trouble and scanned the next room with his lamp. Predictably it was the decontamination chamber required by all high-level biosafety labs, equipped with evacuation fans, showers, and UV sterilizers. He was still as dangerously far from the new floor on that side, but the shower doors were just below him, like a platform. He lowered himself warily. They groaned, but took his weight.

He walked across to the far door, which was hinged on what was now the upper edge. Normally Control would never allow both doors of a decontamination chamber to be open at the same time, but here Control was dead. With the hinges at the top, the flap hung ajar, prevented from closing by a strip of scrap lithium alloy bent over the jamb.

He gently pushed the door wider and peered through. The next room had been the biologists' dorm, equipped with fold-away bunks and a few more conveniences. Linen, clothes, and mattresses had fallen in heaps against the starboard side, and on this clutter lay a dying woman. She was understandably naked in the heat, but had pulled a towel over herself in an attempt at modesty. One hand covered her eyes to shield them from his lamp, and the other held the bottle she had used for tapping. It was empty, of course. Her effort to speak made only a croaking sound.

He turned the lamp so it shone upward. "Hi." Careful to prop the door behind him, he climbed down one of the foldaway bunks, which was still chained to the wall and served as a ladder.

"My name's Seth Broderick. I'm from Mighty Mite's *Golden Hind*, and we're going to take you home." He knelt, pulling his spare water bottle from his pouch. He needed that water himself. It would fit safely to his drinking tube, but once he broke the seal to let this woman drink from it he would not be able to use it without being exposed to biohazard. He broke the seal, lifted her with an arm under her shoulders, and put the tube to her mouth.

She was either the master or the astrobiologist. She had been marooned down here for more than two weeks and he was going to rescue her. Cacafuego's perils now seemed less dangerous.

According to Duddridge, she had been hallucinating and suffering from a high fever, but she did not look fevered now. The killer planet might still be a serpent with two heads, but it had a weak bite if this woman had survived so long in these conditions. She must be a very tough lady.

"That's enough for now," Seth said, removing the bottle and letting her lie down. "Have you been drinking the muck outside, or has the shuttle's supply just run out?"

She mumbled, "Two days ago."

"Are you Mariko or Meredith?"

"Meredith."

That was often a herm name and she was large, with curves that suggested muscle more than fat, but Seth decided she was probably trad female. That instinct to cover her nudity was not herm, and she wore her hair longer than most herms did. He spread the towel better and grinned through his vizor at her. She smiled back. He opened the first aid packet on his suit, loaded the injector with a stim shot, and squirted it into her arm.

"We named the river after you. Galactic ran away, you know?"

"So… should you. Go! Virus…"

"No." He did not believe in infective agents that could slip through modern biosafety barriers. No virus particle or bacterium would penetrate his suit.

"Prospector to *Golden Hind*. Can you read me?"

Silence. The metal skin of the shuttle was blocking the feeble signals from his helmet. He wanted to know how the storm was progressing. He needed the shuttle more urgently now.

"You haven't starved, though," he said. The galley would have held emergency rations, but could she have reached it? The corridor door, the original exit, was three meters overhead, and closed. She must have been confined to this room and the laboratory. The decon showers might have let her access the water store.

"The centaurs bring me food," she whispered.

Pause for thought. Wildcatters were always inventing weird names for new things, but he could not help wondering if her hallucinations lingered on. After three weeks in this atmosphere she must have serious nitrogen narcosis, at least, even if she had recovered whatever virus or bacillus she had caught before. Anything she said might be delusion.

Six-toed footprints with talons?

"Centaurs?"

"Amphibious creatures. Like otters."

"Sentient?"

She nodded.

Something had laid a dead fish at her doorstep. Damn! First contact and Mighty Mite would be ruined by it.

"Friendly?"

"They don't like clothes."

Seth decided to leave the sentience question until later. It raised far too many questions and no answers.

"Apart from thirst, how are you feeling?"

"Weak, hungry, and so glad to see a human face that I'm about to have hysterics."

"I often have that effect on people."

"It's against my religion. I was so sure I was going to... I can feel that stim shot working." She took the water bottle from him and drank.

With her solid build, blond hair, and fair skin, she was a Brunhilda, not a Venus. Women were rarely prospectors. The thought that he might have met a female Seth Broderick amused him. As far as he could recall the legends, neither Brunhilda nor her boyfriend had ended happily.

"There's a storm brewing outside. Will we be safe from it in here?"

"Safe as anywhere."

"We have only one shuttle and it can't land until the weather improves. You will have to put up with my company for a few hours."

She smiled for the first time. Under normal conditions, that smile would rank as thrilling. "You won't get very far in that armor, Sir Knight."

"No offense intended, but I wasn't planning any heavy moves just yet. I'll take a rain check. Will you be able to walk to the shuttle when it comes? I doubt I can carry you in this gravity."

"You ought to rescue smaller maidens."

"Or maidens in less distress. How long have you been here?"

"Nineteen-hour days or twenty-four hour? I have no idea."

Why shut herself up in this dark oven? Perhaps because vermin would have trouble getting in. Or perhaps she had just crawled in here at the end to die. Only one hell of a strong-minded woman would still be anywhere close to her right mind after such an ordeal.

"Our ship's calendar won't be yours, of course, but we reckon it's been eighteen days since Duddridge posted his beacon."

"I'd been here five or six days by then," she said.

That was longer than Duddridge had implied in his beacon message. The more lies Seth identified in that, the more he agreed with JC's suspicions that Galactic must have found something worth a double or triple murder. If so, Meredith Tsukuba must know what that something was. This might be a very profitable rescue. Except for the sentience problem.

"And he just pissed off, abandoning you?"

"It was the right decision. I told him to. I confirmed what Mariko had told him; that the infectious agent had bypassed all our barriers and couldn't be contained. We were contagious and too sick to help ourselves. An unmanned shuttle wouldn't be able to rescue us from the wreck, and a manned mission would put other lives at risk. Even if he could get us back upside, we'd endanger the ship's crew."

"It was your idea that he abandon you?"

"Mine and Mariko's. And you should get away from me, too."

This was insane. "You really think that bug of yours can penetrate a K333 suit?"

"Yes. It got through all our defenses. Dylan caught it first. Granted, there's a very slight chance his suit was compromised in the centaur attack. But it didn't say so, and we'd kept him quarantined in the infirmary. Then Mariko came down with it. Then I did."

Seth shifted to a more comfortable position and thought some more about sentient centaurs who left offerings of dead fish. Meredith might still be hallucinating; nothing she said could be trusted. "Whatever it was, you survived, so it isn't fatal. Did it kill the others?"

"Something killed Dylan, but it could have been a combination of the infection and trauma from his fall. I was suffering from muscle spasms and blackouts, so Mariko had strapped me into a bunk. That saved me when the storm waves rolled us. I came to my senses eventually, hung on a wall in here, in the dark. I managed to free myself, but I couldn't find a way to her, wherever she was when it hit." She glanced up at the door that was now in the ceiling. "The outside port hatch won't open and the starboard one is jammed or locked."

"You mean their bodies must still be somewhere in the shuttle?"

She nodded. "I thought I heard knocking for a day or two, but it might have been the wind."

JC would have said "flaming shit!" at that point. *De Soto's* telemetry must have told Duddridge what had happened to the shuttle, but he hadn't mentioned it in his beacon message.

Meredith had survived the rolling, Mariko Seidel might have. If *De Soto* had sent down another manned shuttle with tools, both women might have been rescued. Duddridge was going to be hung, drawn, and quartered in the public media when ISLA released his report. He couldn't edit or suppress his ship's records. Why had he thrown away his career like that? Just because a pair of terrified, delirious women claimed they had succumbed to a virus that could bypass modern biocontainment precautions?

Or was JC right when he said Duddridge had found something on the planet that justified so much treachery?

Seth heard a faint roll of thunder, much muffled by the shuttle walls.

Meredith heard it also. "How long until the storm hits, Prospector?"

"Seth. Seth Broderick. It must be due soon. Can you walk?"

She nodded. "I can crawl. Go and report to your friends."

"What I ought to do is go and find my baggage. It has three more water bottles and we're going to need them. But it will take me a couple of hours, there and back."

"Don't tell me you walked that far over the boulder flats?"

"We didn't know it would be such hard going."

"We did. We had close-ups from the drones. That's why we landed beside this distributary channel. It makes for easy walking all the way to the flower pots."

"*Golden Hind* doesn't carry atmospheric drones," Seth admitted. Drones or not, the fact that Duddridge had ordered the shuttle to set down a good kilometer from the chimneys showed that even Galactic had not been certain that those were natural and not artifacts.

"You mustn't risk it again," Meredith said firmly. "You'll break a leg for sure, or get caught in the storm. And the water you collect won't cover the sweat you'll lose, there and back."

The mere thought of water made Seth thirsty. "What choice do I have?"

"We can collect rainwater, but you'll have to boil it with your blazer, and I honestly don't believe that will sterilize it."

He hadn't brought a blazer.

"That's a last resort. I can dehydrate a bit longer." This shuttle would still contain everything they could possibly need, but they couldn't get at it. *Niagara* would be hours away yet. He stood up, weary all over from the constant gravity overload. "I'll go and report."

"Shine your light around for me. There's a bra about somewhere."

He laughed. "Modesty at a time like this?"

"Necessity in gravity like this."

He apologized and found the bra for her.

⊶ ✴ ⊷

As soon as he clambered through into the laboratory he heard almost continuous thunder. Gusts of rain sweeping across the plain had cut visibility down to a hundred meters or so. His external thermometer told him that the temperature had dropped twenty degrees. He had estimated that he could stand three hours on the surface, but now that seemed hopelessly optimistic and he had a lot more of this ordeal to look forward to. Even after the storm passed, *Golden Hind* might have to wait an hour or two for its orbit to line up with Sombrero before it could launch *Niagara*.

"Prospector to *Golden Hind*. Do you read?"

"*Yes!*" JC bellowed. "What the flaming shit have you been doing for so long?"

"You know how time flies when you're with a pretty girl."

"They're alive?"

"Meredith Tsukuba is. She's suffering from dehydration, malnutrition, probably nitrogen narcosis. Perhaps emotional trauma, but she's a very tough woman."

"What about the comas and hallucinations?"

Seth hadn't made up his mind yet. "Nothing obvious. She'll need a long decompression after this and certainly quarantine."

"Master, this is Jordan."

"Yes, sir."

"Bad news. Prepare for a major storm surge. That hurricane will make landfall right at high tide."

"No problem," Seth said. "Let me restate that: I mean, no decision needed. We're in the shuttle and that's as safe a place as we'll find. Our problem is going to be drinking water. We have none left. We'll try collecting rain; the air is wet enough

98

to swim in right now." If he opened his vizor to take as much as one sip of rainwater, he would be exposed to biohazard and faced with a long quarantine.

He uploaded his plog, bringing *Golden Hind* up to date on his situation and what he had learned. He didn't ask how long the storm would last because he didn't want to hear the answer. The rest of the team came on to wish him luck, or prayer in one case.

The drawer he had noticed earlier was now explained. He dragged it behind him as he crawled out of the cave on hands and knees — the storm had barely started and already he did not dare try to stand up in it. He scooped a hollow in the sand to anchor the drawer; he packed sand in around it. The rain was almost horizontal, but enough was going in to fill it fairly soon.

A good prospector should never miss a chance to sample. Back in the shuttle, he wrapped up some fish bones, a couple of beetles, and some more fecal pellets, larger than those he had found earlier. Those took him past the total of twenty he had promised JC. Now he just had to deliver them.

He headed back to find Meredith. She had reached the decon room, crawling out on hands and knees. She was doing fine, but did not object when he steadied her as she climbed down into the former lab. In addition to the bra, she wore a bed sheet as a sort of sarong.

"I have always believed that women look sexiest in garments that promise to fall off at any moment."

"Sexy? If you think I look sexy in my present condition, you really are deprived. Close your eyes."

"Not likely!" He turned his back instead.

Meredith draped the sheet over him in case he cheated. She crawled outside for a brief needle shower. Once she was dressed again, still wet but not chilled in the muggy heat, they made themselves as comfortable as possible, sitting on the lab table that stood half buried in sand. As a bench it was awkwardly tilted and not high enough for Seth's legs, but it beat standing.

Her hair was still a tangled disaster and her long ordeal certainly showed, but a few days' decent diet, some grooming, and something daring to wear, and she would turn all the heads in the dance hall. Her face was broad, showing the bone, portraying strength, not grace. Her eyes were large and steady, very pale gray. She was an Amazon.

"A steak about this size," she said. "Rare. Fried onions, fried yams, and a magnum of ice-cold champagne. To celebrate my rescue."

"Is that the biggest steak available?" He realized he was ravenous.

"And decent rags. And a comb, fergawsake."

"Indecent rags have their good side." He was amazed by her courage. What she had been through would have reduced most people to gibbering idiots, and it wasn't over yet. "There's a dead fish outside."

"They go stinky very fast in the heat."

With a roar like the end of several worlds, the rain turned to hail. Stones the size of eyeballs thundered on the shuttle, many bouncing in through the gap. In that gravity they would have battered Seth to pulp if they had caught him out in the open, going to fetch the water from his packs. The cataclysm stopped after ten minutes or so, and he recovered the drawer, pulling it inside. Meredith was waiting with a cup.

"*Votre champagne, madame.* Steak to follow." The hail should melt quickly in the tropical-type heat. Outside, rain and thunder continued. The shuttle trembled as ever-stronger gusts hit the remaining wing.

"I was warned that there's a storm surge on the way," he said.

Meredith pulled a face. "We may have to go back inside, then. I've seen water almost high enough to flood through into the decon room. If it gets past that, we could be in some trouble."

He wondered if the whole shuttle could shift, maybe break apart; didn't say so.

"And the centaurs will come visiting," she said. "They may bring me fish, but if they see you in that suit, they'll go for you. That's what they did to Dylan." She sipped rainwater.

At this point Reese would say that it wasn't the centaurs that bothered him, it was the unicorns.

Seth said, "While we're waiting, and if you're up to it, I'd like to record your account of what happened from the time you landed on Cacafuego."

"That's what you call it? I like our name better. But I'll try."

"Prospector to *Golden Hind*. Can you hear us over the racket?"

Maria's voice. "Barely, but Control can filter the background out later."

"Ok. We're twiddling thumbs here. It's raining on our picnic. I have Prospector Meredith Tsukuba with me, and she's going to tell us what went wrong for Galactic's landing party."

"If I tell you what went right," Meredith said. "It will be quicker."

DAYS 375 TO 390

001.196 SENTIENT means a creature or species exhibiting at least two of the following features:

[a] deliberate use of fire,

[b] manufacture of tools for later use,

[c] regulation of social interaction by language,

[d] an ability to communicate abstract concepts,

[e] evidence of art, religion, or rituals other than sexual or territorial display.

001.197 SEMI-SENTIENT means a creature or species exhibiting only one of the above features.

General Regulations
InterStellar Licensing Authority
2375 edition

"When ISLA's report on GK79986B came out," Meredith said, "everyone got very excited and also furious that Mighty Mite had cheated and jumped the gun. Galactic rammed us through our final prep in record time and we left orbit just a few days after you did. The scuttlebutt was that Galactic had told Old Doddery not to spare the horses. So he didn't. We squandered a lot of ferrets on the way — I mean we didn't wait for them all to return, so our navigators could choose the safest possible haven to aim for in the next jump. That's standard procedure, of course, but what I heard was that as soon as one came back with readings that met minimum safety standards, we took that route and jumped, abandoning any probes that returned later. We entered orbit around Hesperides on our *Day 354*, right about Hesperides' northern summer solstice. I don't know what that date would be by your ship's calendar, but we knew we had won, because there was no sign of you, the Mighty Mite Pirates."

Seth said, "We estimated that the solstice had been about our *Day 380*, more than a month ago now. Either we hit more time slip or you beat us by about a month and a half. Your commodore must have cut quite a few corners. When *Golden Hind* files its report, ISLA may take a hard look at his log. And he's going to face very hard questioning about abandoning you."

"I have enough troubles of my own right now, thank you," she said. "We were disappointed by the axial tilt, but some sideways worlds have been profitable, and we were determined to stake it before you did. Then our scanners turned up the flower pots. Know what I mean?"

"We called them chimneys."

"We sent atmospheric drones down to overfly a couple of the colonies and we saw pseudo-mammalian fauna around them. We were thrown into a tizzy. Now we call them centaurs and in my opinion they're sentient."

Oh! "Not just semi-sentient?"

"We weren't sure then, but since I've got to know them better, I'm convinced they're sentient."

"They use tools? Or they have language?"

Meredith shrugged. "Both. GenRegs are vague on this topic, as I'm sure you know. Taken literally, their definitions would qualify crows or parrots as intelligent. People are still arguing how sentient gorillas were, yet ISLA blithely expects a few stressed people to make a correct decision on species no one has ever seen before, and get it right first time."

"ISLA wants to give any possible sentients the benefit of the doubt."

"That's not the way big corporations think. We sent down three drones in all, and every one of them ran afoul of the weather. You can avoid the obvious storms, but there's a lot of CAT about, clear air turbulence."

Seth recalled that Commodore Duddridge, in his beacon message, had claimed to have sent down "a lot" of drones, not just three. Had he lied to his own shuttle crew, so they would not be put off attempting a landing, or to the beacon, hoping to scare *Golden Hind* away when it arrived? He had never mentioned the chimneys or centaurs. His view of the truth was patchy and astigmatic.

"Doddery called for volunteers. Up jumped a dozen suicidal idiots. He picked me and I chose my crew. The three of us came downside on *Day 360*. We chose this site for several reasons, one being that it doesn't get as hot as most of the northern hemisphere landmasses, yet it isn't what on Earth we'd call arctic. Here the equator is the arctic, but there seems to be no permanent ice this far north. It had a fairly typical colony of flower … chimneys, you called them. As usual, they were close to the sea and a river, although I suspect now the river may be incidental. The drones' videos had warned us that the estuary terrain was virtually impassable, but they had also shown some distributary channels like this one. We hoped that they might act as freeways for us wobbly bipeds."

Meredith paused to take another sip of ice water. In her dehydrated and half-starved condition, she was over-reacting to the stim shot, talking fast, going hyper. Weeks of loneliness were showing, too. She might eventually collapse, and then how would Seth ever get her aboard *Niagara* when it returned? She ought to be in a hospital bed cocooned in IV tubes.

Seth said, "Of course you chose to land well back from the chimneys in case they turned out to be a housing project and your shuttle scared a tribe of sentients into starting a religion."

"You guessed it. ISLA would have bust our pretty little asses. We didn't want to waste any time, though. We knew the weather wasn't reliable. As soon as we landed, Dylan Guinizelli and I suited up and headed out. It was a gorgeous day, all blue sky and fluffy clouds. The sun was very low and not oppressive. I really wished I could take my helmet off and smell such a beautiful world. We headed seaward, collecting, dictating, commenting, just like a school field trip.

"We followed the dry channel all the way to the chimneys. They looked bigger than I'd expected, about ten meters high and maybe five across, house-sized. But they're irregular, obviously a natural growth, something like algal mounds. Their outsides are rough, like coral, and they taper upward, though not so much that you'd call them cones. On Earth you could climb them easily. Here, even Dylan, who's … who *was* a hell-raiser, a crazy man, reckless to the point of insanity… Can you believe he enjoyed blindfold mountain climbing? Escorted, of course, but even so… Even Dylan wasn't inclined to try climbing anything in this gravity."

Dylan might have been a fun guy to know. Had Meredith found him so? Again she paused to drink and Seth spoke up, just to let her rest.

"You said that the centaurs take shelter inside them. You must have seen that from the drones, but our equipment couldn't show us so much detail. We weren't even sure that they were hollow. I know from what we did see that they are littoral, growing only in tidal areas, and Cacafuego has a lot of those. So if they're plants or giant barnacles, not houses, what's their game? How do they make a living?"

"You are terrestrializing!" she said. "You know how rarely our Earthly categories fit exobiology. Oysters have feathers and bats with hooves and so on. I think coral might be a better analogy, and coral isn't a plant. If they trap and poison marine life, like sea anemones do, then they obviously don't hurt the centaurs. Mariko suggested that they might collect rainwater. The rainfall here is stupendous, as you can see."

"Quite." Outside their little cave the water was coming down in ropes, with visibility reduced to a few meters. So far the sand had absorbed it, but Seth was watching the pond, and now it was spreading fast. The wind came in hurricane gusts, shaking the shuttle, making his ears pop. There could be no question of sending for *Niagara* until the weather lifted. He was very thirsty. "You suppose the centaurs use the chimneys to collect rainwater?"

"I wouldn't say 'use.' They don't build the pots, but they seem to make use of them. At some seasons, the precipitation must be high enough to keep the chimneys full of fresh or brackish water. The contrast between saltwater outside and fresh inside during high tide could serve as an energy source, either by osmotic pressure or by some electrolytic process. Or they may just ooze water to keep cool during low tide, when the sun is strong. Mariko suggested later that the chimneys and the centaurs could have a symbiotic thing going. The chimneys provide the centaurs with storm shelters, and the centaurs' droppings fertilize the chimneys.

But they are hollow, they are largely full of water, and they let centaurs play house, as we then discovered.

"We decided to return to the shuttle. That was when things started to go wrong. We had explored a little over one klick of a whole planet but we were beat! I admit it."

"I understand," Seth said, with feeling.

"We had just turned back when a centaur popped its head out of one of the flower pots and started jabbering like crazy. The others obviously heard it, so they couldn't have had their heads underwater. They have no gills — they breathe air, but I suppose the pots aren't quite full of water. They must come up to breathe but we certainly hadn't noticed them doing so. Right away a whole herd of them appeared. Two or three to every chimney, they scrambled down the sides and came after us.

"Dylan was closer than I was and got the worst of it. He had time to draw his stun gun and get off a few shots, but there were far too many of them. They swarmed him. I was farther away, and I drove them off with firecrackers."

ISLA was going to hit the roof over that. Galactic would have to prove beyond any reasonable doubt that the Cacafuego centaurs were not sentient. Even then, it might be fined for using such weapons when it could not have been sure of the centaurs' status. So company policy must be *no* sentience, which explained why *De Soto* had not posted a purple flag.

"Teeth? Claws? Weapons?"

"They have claws on their walking feet, but their hands are wrap-around flippers that may not be as prehensile as ours but can grasp things at least as well as an elephant's trunk can. Some of them were carrying fishing spears, but they didn't use them against us. First they tugged at Dylan's suit. Then they tried to cut it with sharp stones and implements like daggers. I learned later that those are teeth from something like a shark. We were recording, of course, and later Control analyzed their speech patterns and concluded that their noises were more than just a series of alarm calls, but possibly not a true language. Our best estimate was that the centaurs rank about whale or dolphin level in communication. We could also analyze their actions, and Control was confident to the ninety-eighth percentile that the critters were not trying to hurt Dylan. They were only trying to free him from his suit. If you're an air-breathing aquatic species, your greatest danger may lie in getting tangled in weeds, so they have an instinctive response to help anyone in that predicament. Or the orange color may signify some dangerous predator. Whatever the logic, they seemed to see him as a giant cub in peril and the whole tribe came to the rescue."

Jordan's voice. *"Golden Hind* to Prospector."

"Just a moment," Seth told Meredith, who couldn't hear his helmet speaker. "Come in, *Golden Hind.*"

"Storm surge on the way. Expect flooding in about fifteen minutes and the crest ten or fifteen after that. We can't predict the depth, I'm afraid."

"Call up a plan of a KR745."

"Got it."

"The bird's lying on its port side. We're sitting in the lab, where the fuselage is almost broken apart. If we get flooded out, we'll retreat through the decon room to the biologists' dormitory. We can't go beyond that, but we can shut ourselves in. There ought to be enough air in there for a couple of hours. If we're underwater much longer than that, have a nice flight home, ok?"

"We're praying for you." So even Jordan was into prayer mode now.

Seth signed off and reported the bad news to Meredith. The water table was rising, bringing the pond almost to the door of their cave. He was thirsty. For the first time he seriously wondered if this killer planet might be going to claim another victim.

There was nothing he could do about that now, except wait and see. His duty was to continue getting Meredith's story into *Golden Hind*'s record, because the odds were that she wouldn't come out of this alive either. Her testimony would be invaluable if Mighty Mite and Galactic ended up in court.

Which they likely would. Seth didn't care about JC and his moneyed buddies. JC Lecanard already had what he wanted — the video of Seth planting the flag and the two samples Seth had sent back with the shuttle. If Prospector Broderick did not come back alive, he could not claim his danger bonus, but JC could stake the planet and file for a development license, arguing that Galactic's quarantine beacon was premature. If ISLA accepted that Mighty Mite deserved another try, it might grant at least a provisional license. Then Galactic would have to meet his price. Or JC could cut Galactic out, find other financing, build a better shuttle, and come back later. Of course Galactic would try to bury Mighty Mite under a landslide of litigation — sue, appeal, delay, argue, and spend them into bankruptcy. That was how the game was played.

As long as ISLA did not judge the centaurs to be an intelligent species.

Screw them all. Seth had little desire to help JC, but he did want to help the rest of the crew, who also had a stake in the expedition. A potential action for murder against Commander Duddridge might keep Galactic out of the courts.

Seth felt as beat as he had after the worst fights of his pugilism career. "Next episode? Dylan had just been knocked down for his own good."

"The fall broke his arm. He was really pissed about that, the first fracture he'd ever had. He also got bruises, of course, but nothing more. We headed back to *Mercury*. That's what I'd named the shuttle. Some centaurs followed us for a while, but they like to keep their hides damp, so they soon ran off.

"Then the second shoe fell. We were in sight of the shuttle. Out of clear air and blue sky came a blast of wind. It knocked us both flat, which didn't help Dylan's arm. It lifted *Mercury* half off the ground and dropped it. Two legs crumpled and one of the jets was badly bent. Our bird was a dead duck.

"Mariko reported upstairs at once of course. *Courageous* began fueling its shuttle. Before it was ready to come and get us, a real storm blew in. We were stuck here overnight."

"Broken legs and jets? That was all the damage to the shuttle?"

"That time. Dylan was in serious pain after the second fall. I had to help him back to the *Mercury*. He weighed a thousand kilos, but we got there, and I got him into the EVA decon. And we cut no corners! Old Doddery didn't want to believe me, later, but we went through the full sterilization treatment, every bit of it. Dylan was weeping with the pain in his arm, but I insisted we stand there for the entire fifteen-minute cleansing. I swear to you that there was not one single microbe or virus particle left on our suits!"

"I believe you," Seth said, not entirely truthfully. The toughest test an EVA suit ever had to survive was the returning disinfection, and yet something had contaminated the shuttle. He wondered if the shuttle itself might have been breached in the fall. Control should have reported loss of the over-pressure needed to keep out biohazards, but the electronics might have been damaged also.

"At that time we couldn't be certain that his suit had not been punctured, so Mariko and I put him in the quarantine room. She got his suit off of him and treated him as well as she could. His arm was a mess, but she deadened it and did a rough set, all we could manage."

The KR745 shuttle was a flying hotel. *Niagara* had no quarantine room, and the Gut doubled as EVA decon area.

"Did you test his suit?"

"Don't you try and tell me my job, Seth Whatever-your-name-is. I may be blonde but I am not dumb! You beat me out for the Mighty Mite job, but Galactic hired me ahead of four hundred other applicants. Yes, I tested both suits, just like GenRegs say. I inflated them both and neither lost a millibar of pressure in the next eight hours. They had not been compromised in any way. Next morning Dylan was going in and out of convulsions and delirium."

"Concussion?" Seth guessed.

"Could be, but concussion doesn't make you run a fever of forty-one degrees. Granted a shuttle med-kit is not the highest of high-techs, but it did have his blood sample and it did report mild concussion, but mainly it was screaming *Unknown Infective Agent*. Dylan was a big guy. When he went into convulsions, Mariko had to tie him down. We tried every antibiotic and antiviral we had without success.

"The weather was hellish all day. By nightfall, Earth time — we have no real darkness here yet — Mariko was running a fever too. That's another mystery. She was a biologist, fergawsake, so she knew all about biohazard. She'd tended Dylan by the book, wearing her lab aseptic suit, showering... Her infection is just as hard to explain as his was.

"That was our *Day 363*, I think. By the next day I had them both tied to their bunks, Dylan still in the quarantine room, Mariko in the biologists' dorm. By noon, ship time, I felt shitty-awful. The med-kit diagnosed an unknown infective agent. At that point there was no point my trying to preserve asepsis. I was starting to worry. Duddridge was talking of sending down an unmanned shuttle, but I couldn't carry even Mariko in this gravity, and Dylan would need a crane. In any case, squalls kept coming through, so the shuttle never launched. There may have been a storm surge or a very high tide, because the ponds rose, and I had centaur visitors bouncing around the outside of the shuttle, warbling away. I did not open the door."

"Inhospitable of you."

"Very. I napped for an hour or so. When I awoke, Mariko was hallucinating and Dylan had died. My memory gets a bit fuzzy around then.

"It was likely the next day when I found I was tied to a bunk in the biologist's dorm and Mariko was looking after me, although she could barely walk, she was so dizzy. She kept telling me were both going to die."

"Commander Duddridge reported that an unmanned shuttle was sent down about then, but it crashed."

"I spoke to him and he told me that, but we saw no signs of it. I don't know what day it was when the storm surge came and I found myself turning cartwheels in bed and *Mercury* ended up on its side like this. All systems dead. I've told you the rest. Dammit, someone's been sandblasting my throat."

"Take a break. You've done very well."

DAY 413, CONTINUED

002.001 When any expedition, whether exploratory or development, has significant reason to believe it has encountered a sentient species, it must immediately:

[a] terminate all contact with that species,

[b] discontinue sampling,

[c] withdraw all personnel, equipment, refuse, and all signs of its presence,

[d] post a Sentience Alert Beacon as defined in001.874.

General Regulations
InterStellar Licensing Authority
2375 edition

⊷⊨⊙ ✳ ⊙⊨⊶

The pond was washing into the cave with every wave. That water must be fresh, although it was certainly not sterile. There was no sign of a break in the torrential rain.

"Prospector to *Golden Hind*."

"Go ahead, Seth." It was JC himself on watch.

"There's no chance of rescue for at least three hours, and eight or ten is more likely. I'm dehydrated. I'm going to open my vizor and drink some of the rainwater that's slopping around outside. Plan to quarantine both of us when you get us back."

"Seth, that's suicide!"

"It's sensible. Meredith's alive and well, and it sounds as if Mariko survived until after the second crash, so whatever infection they caught wasn't fatal. Once that storm surge arrives, there won't be any fresh water anywhere. Prospector out."

"No!" JC was not easily dismissed. "Listen. Collect some water by all means, but don't drink it until you're truly desperate."

"Good idea," Seth said, although he knew he couldn't last another five or six hours without the dehydration affecting his physical and mental state. Dehydration brought on cramps, dizziness, delirium and a lot of other things he could not afford if he was going to get out of this mess alive.

"And Reese wants a word with you."

"Seth? This is Reese."

"Hi, Reese."

"Those samples you sent up... No signs of reversed chirality. The proteins are terrestrial-normal."

"So it was just the sort of stupid idea only a Neanderthal like me would think of. Thanks. Prospector out."

"Come and sit down, Neanderthal," Meredith said.

He obeyed. "So tell me the rest of your story." Anything to take his mind off his thirst.

"Nothing to tell. By the next day I was feeling much better, thinking more clearly, but I knew I was doomed to die here. I could get water from the taps in the decon room but no food. I thought I heard Mariko tapping sometimes. I tried tapping back, but her response never seemed to make any sense, so perhaps I was just hearing a loose piece of the hull blown around by the wind. It stopped after a couple of days.

"When I was strong enough, I crawled out here, to the lab. I renamed it the lanai. I had no way of calling *De Soto* or the other ships. I tried to mark out a signal on the sand, because by then I'd decided that the infection wasn't always fatal. It probably killed Dylan, I wasn't sure about Mariko, and I seemed to be recovering."

"*De Soto* was still there, then?"

"They all were. They were in very low orbit, and sometimes, when the sun was behind a cloud, I could see sunlight reflected off them as they went by overhead. Always there would be at least one of the three. Then they closed up into a group, close together, and I knew they were about to leave. Then I saw their jump flash. And knew I was alone."

"Did you write your message in the sand?"

"It was very faint. I did drag a chair outside to show that there was still someone alive. They either didn't see it, or they ignored it. The centaurs took it away later."

Seth tried to imagine what the media would do with this story, but it made his mind reel. Duddridge was a dead man walking. He would be torn to shreds.

"That must have been almost three weeks ago."

"Feels like three years. Now you turn up. I may start weeping soon."

"Weep away. Trauma and stim shorts can do that to anyone. You'll be an international celebrity, you know. Sell your memoirs for a fortune."

She leaned against him. It was a romantic gesture, except that she weighed a ton. "You really think this damned world will let us go?"

He put an arm around her. "I think the wind's dropping already. As soon as the storm lets up, *Niagara* will come for us. We'll walk over, load the samples, and be on our way."

"You're sweet," she said dreamily.

She must be more confused than he'd realized. No one had called Seth Broderick sweet in the last twenty years.

He took Meredith's cup and went over to the mouth of the cave. After one last breath of pure air, he removed his helmet, ignoring Control's squawks of protest. The roar of the storm grew louder. Cacafuego smelled of steam, and sea, and something that he thought might be mulch. Despite the rain, the air was hotter than a sauna, provoking instant beads of perspiration on his face. He filled the cup where a steady trickle of water was running down the side of the shuttle. He drank.

"This hemlock tastes like champagne."

Meredith smiled. "Champagne is iced. If it's warm, it's hemlock." She stared at his face until he wondered what she was thinking. Then she said, "I didn't know Neanderthals were so good looking."

She was probably joking, but stim shots could have strange effects on people, especially if they were seriously traumatized, as she was. He drank another cupful.

"Beauty is in the eye of the beholder. You'd have been happy to see Quasimodo or one of his gargoyles."

"Come and sit by me, Quasimodo. Why not take off your bell-ringing costume first?"

She must know what men wore inside an EVA suit, but she was right. The suit's temperature control wouldn't work without the helmet, so in this heat he must either remove the suit or put his helmet back on.

"I think I may as well die in comfort. But I'll undress in the bedroom, if you don't mind. My gear will be safer there." The larger waves were coming well inside now, lapping close to the table. The castaways might soon have to abandon the lab and retreat to the dorm.

"Right. You go and slip into something comfortable," she said.

Not knowing her, he wasn't sure how much she was playacting or what he would do if she started making serious advances. Under normal circumstances he wouldn't hesitate, for she was an attractive woman, but in their current predicament there was something grotesque about the idea. He had given her drugs, which would make it feel like date rape.

"Here," he said, detaching the communicator and camera from his helmet. He handed to them on their strap, which could be worn as a headband. "You talk to the nice people upstairs."

He clambered back into the decon room and crawled across the unsteady shower doors to the dorm. There, far from the raging storm, the air stank of rotting fish and human sweat. He removed his suit by the light of his helmet, stripping down to shorts and shoes. He was glad to be rid of the heavy suit, but now perspiration was pouring off him and he would need to drink much more water.

He had just begun to retrace his path when he heard a strange *yittering* noise ahead. He crawled forward across the shower doors as quietly as he could.

A herd of centaurs had arrived. Meredith had shed her bra and sarong. She was kneeling in the water that now sloshed to and fro in the former laboratory, moving her hands in a *feed-me* gesture, and the visitors were milling around her, as noisy as excited parakeets. Those closest to her kept fondling her hair.

They were about the size of middling dogs, black on top and white below, in the manner of penguins or fish, but their skin was as smooth as dolphins'. Like the lizard Seth had caught hours ago, they had six limbs, which must be the standard for Cacafuego's vertebrate equivalents. They walked on the rear four limbs, but their front torsos bent upward, so that the first set of limbs looked like arms and their head faced forward, in human fashion. It was easy to see why Meredith and her team had named them centaurs.

Their hands had no fingers, being shaped like giant tongues, able to roll up to grip things. He saw three or four centaurs with spears and others carrying gourds, which must be used for storage or transport. The way they waved their hands about in gestures seemed typically human, but their faces were quite alien. The closest model he could think of would be giant pandas with muzzles full of sharp teeth. Fangs would not penetrate an EVA suit, and they were not being used to attack or even threaten Meredith. Sentient or not, centaurs were cute. They might make popular pets, except that ISLA would never allow an advanced species to be imported. ISLA wouldn't hesitate to call them sentient.

Did he? Maybe. He didn't *want* them to be intelligent! Although these hexapods would certainly qualify as intelligent by ISLA's muddled rules, they were not building nuclear power plants yet, and their descendants never would. By terrestrial standards they were obviously marine mammals. The first step to technology was fire, and their chances of encountering that, let alone taming it, must be very close to zero.

As a first guess, this harsh sideways world would force them to migrate north and south with the sun. If permanent sea ice at the equator made that impossible, most likely they hibernated. The chimneys might serve as their winter lairs.

Well aware that Meredith would accuse him of terrestrializing again, Seth decided that *Centaurus cacafuegensis* was closer to marsupial than placental. Their white chests showed no nipples. Several bore humps on their backs with tiny centaur heads protruded from them, like baby kangaroos in their mothers' pouches. But centaurs also had a resemblance to flying squirrels, because a web of skin joined all three limbs on each side. The general effect was that of a blanket draped over their backs, and very long sleeves in front. Their walk was an awkward roll, but they would be powerful swimmers, flying through water as bats flew through air. They had quadrupeds' stability on land, plus bipeds' dexterity. They had sharp teeth and claws to catch fish. Their overall design seemed more efficient than anything on Earth or any other planet Seth could recall offhand. Exobiologists would go into raptures over them.

His doubts about their intelligence faded when a centaur outside the cave started yittering louder than the others, and the crowd parted to let it enter. Unsteady under the load of a meter-long fish held in its hand flaps, the newcomer advanced to Meredith and presented her with its still-twitching gift. The rest of them yittered in loud approval and applauded by slapping their flippers, like seals. That was language Seth was hearing, and the speakers were a wild species, not trained or domesticated. Their behavior was closer to a demonstration of sentience than anything witnessed in a century of human stellar exploration. Centaurs met at least three of the five criteria in *GenRegs 001.196 [C]*. *Golden Hind*'s report would kill any hope of a development license.

So now JC's suspicion about Duddridge made a lot of sense. There was more than enough evidence here to post a purple beacon on Cacafuego, and that would have sent *Golden Hind* away with its tail between its legs. Instead he had posted the quarantine flag, which might have seemed equally justified but which would not by itself have barred Galactic from sending a second expedition in future. He had passed up a chance at eternal fame in favor of a chance to return. Why? What opportunity for profit had he seen on this brutal world that Seth was missing?

While Meredith was thanking the centaurs for their kindness, Seth realized that she was not wearing the communicator headband he had given her, their only link to *Golden Hind*. Furthermore, a couple of youngish-looking centaurs were playing tug-of-war with his precious sample bag. Any moment they would pull it open and all his hard work would be lost forever.

"Hey!" he yelled. "Stop that!" He swung his feet over the door. On Earth he would have jumped. On Cacafuego, he had to clamber down as carefully as some fragile old lady.

The cave erupted in a tumult of yittering, a centaur panic. They had not known there was another of the monsters up there watching them, a larger version of the one they knew. A human crowd would have fled out the door in terror. The centaurs swarmed, but they headed for Seth himself, and their cries seemed to be more alarm calls than threats. The claws on their middle and rear paws enable them to climb, after a fashion. Some scrambled up the makeshift workbench-ladder beside him. Flippers wrapped around his ankles, arms clasped his waist, and he was dragged loose. Only the knee-deep water and a layer of centaurs saved him from serious injury.

He emerged spluttering but unharmed except for bruises, and none of his would-be rescuers seemed to have been damaged either. They must have rubber bones. They had not done with him yet. A dozen flippers grabbed his shorts and ripped them away in shreds. Other centaurs boiled around his legs to get those dangerous shoes off him. He was tipped back in the water again. Only when he was safely mother-naked was he allowed to sit up. Conscious of Meredith's stare, he preferred not to stand.

"All right?" she said, having to shout.

"Where is the communicator?" he yelled, but couldn't make out her answer over the storm outside and the excitement inside. The centaurs were fascinated by hair. *And this new one had it on his chest, too!* Then they discovered the stubble on his chin and every one of them wanted to stroke that, so that he could hardly breathe for flippers. He arranged his thighs to protect other places.

The waves were growing larger, threatening to float him, and already floating the centaurs. He wanted to move both himself and Meredith to the watertight compartments, but now that he knew that the centaurs could climb, he did not want to give them the idea of exploring in there. They were as curious as monkeys, another sign of intelligence.

A glimpse of orange through the forest of flippers and bright-eyed panda-like faces reminded him of the sample bag he had come to rescue. He heaved himself to his feet. The juvenile gang had given up their tug-of-war and taken to tossing the bag around in a game of catch. Seth struggled in their direction through water and massed centaurs. The excitement had begun to die a little, but revelation of more of him raised the noise level again. *The alien had hairy legs!*

"Mine!" he roared and tried to grab the sample bag. That made the game even better. The bag hurtled past him several times, but his terrestrial reflexes couldn't judge the higher speeds involved and he floundered, making a fool of himself and starting to lose his temper. He could recognize laughter, even in Centaur, and he thought he heard some human mirth in there also. At last, more by luck than skill, he intercepted a pass and retrieved the precious bag.

He raised it over his head. "Mine!" he repeated. They had gourds and spears; they must understand the concept of property. Yes, but that might not be the point in this case.

The teenager-equivalents thought this was another game and tried to jump high enough to reach the prize. He staggered as they collided with him and fell back, but he kept possession of the bag. Their yittering changed, growing even shriller. Seth couldn't understand their chatter or their facial expressions, but when one of them slapped him on the chest he understood. Those flippers stung like a hard leather strap. Then another struck his back. He was rescued from a mobbing by one of the spear-carriers, who shouted and scolded, and drove the gang away from the monster.

Seth thanked him and bowed.

He, or she, yittered and clapped flappers.

The dialogue might have progressed further, had it not been interrupted by shrill cries from centaurs outside the cave. Those near the door took it up, and in moments the entire tribe had disappeared.

"That's the surge coming," Meredith said. "Hear the rumble?"

Mostly Seth could still hear the roar of the wind and rain, but at least he no longer had to shout over the centaurs as well. "What happened to the communicator?"

"I was kneeling on it." She struggled to her feet, clutching the headband. She put it on. "Can you hear me? Yes, we're both all right. Sorry to scare you. I had to hide the com from the centaurs. They'll grab anything; worse than jackdaws or keas. Seth's here, see? Yes, I agree. A bit on the hairy side, but that impressed the centaurs."

"Mine!" Seth said firmly, dropping the sample bag so he could relieve Meredith of the com and camera. "Prospector to *Golden Hind.*"

"Welcome back, Mr. Universe," said Hanna. *Oh, Lord, why did it have to be Hanna?* "That storm surge is almost upon you. If you can take cover, do so right now."

"Yes, ma'am. Prospector out."

Seth hurled the sample bag at the doorway to the decon room. He aimed very high and scored at the first attempt. By then he had decided that Meredith would need help and he would be better able to provide it if he went first, however ungallant that seemed. He scrambled up the improvised ladder as fast as he could and reached down for her.

She handed him the fish the centaurs had brought her, rescued her bra just before it floated out the door, and started to climb.

The help he could give her was very limited, and they might not have made it had the rapidly rising water not lifted her. He hauled her in beside him.

Meredith scrambled across the shower doors. He followed. By the time he reached the far side, the water was spilling into the decon chamber. He slid open a panel to let the big shower cubicle take the first of the flood while he made his escape through the second doorway and found a safe foothold on the foldaway bunk that served as a ladder. He let the door latch itself. Then he scrambled down, landing hard on his bare feet. The dormitory was blessedly quiet, the roar of the storm barely detectable through the hull.

He wished he'd saved a reserve of rainwater.

⇥ ✳ ⇤

In the gloom, lit only by his helmet lamp, Meredith sat on the tumbled bedding, making herself more decent with another sheet. Seth looked around for another, absurdly conscious of the vivid red welts where the centaur had slapped him. Fortunately the camera had not recorded that foolish brawl.

"That door is a devil to open," Meredith remarked. Her calmness would have been incredible if he did not suspect she was slipping into some sort of shock.

"Not if the room beyond it is full of water, it won't be." He straightened out another mattress for himself.

"You don't happen to have a blazer on you?"

"Didn't bring one."

"Then I'll eat sushi. Lend me your knife."

Seth wasn't tempted to join her for dinner. He was too parched to eat anything, but he did accept a fragment of Cacafuegian salmon for his sample bag.

"Why bother?" Meredith said with her mouth full. "'Indigenous materials from a world inhabited by sentients must be surrendered to an authorized representative of ISLA.'"

True. "I promised JC I'd collect samples for him. If he wants to deep-space them, that's his privilege."

He left the light on, because his battery had at least ten hours' power remaining, longer than the air in the cabin would last. The shuttle shuddered again as another wave struck it, even bounced slightly. Neither of them commented.

"How does it taste?"

"Excellent," she said with her mouth full. "Needs some Tartar sauce." She ate two slices of raw fish, wrapped the rest in a pillowcase and tucked it away, out of sight or scent. It might be stinking up the dormitory, but the dormitory already reeked of too many things for one more to matter.

By then Seth had noted that the noise of the storm had stopped altogether and the cabin was starting to shift uneasily, both observations suggesting that the shuttle must be almost submerged.

He said, "Since no one can overhear us here and you trust me like you would your own mother, tell me about Commodore Duddridge."

"Of course I trust you, Mom, but you're recording everything we say."

"Then pretend I'm Grandma."

"That's worse. What about Commodore Duddridge?"

"Do you trust him?"

"As much as I trust any bottom-line, bottom-feeding lowlife. I told him so, the last time we spoke, just before the shuttle rolled. I told him things I'd been wanting to say for a long time."

"What sort of things?"

"Well he asked me a lot of personal questions, about my experience with various guys in the crew. *Really* personal details about their technique and performance. So I felt at liberty to tell him how much better in bed they all were than he was and how most anyone aboard would make a better commodore. I told him I expected he would blame the disaster on me. I wanted to get that into the record. He assured me that he would see that no blame attached to me for what happened to the landing party."

"And you didn't believe him?"

"Never!" Meredith moved as if seeking a more comfortable position. No position was comfortable for long in 1.62 gees. "Old Doddery is old for deep-space work and angling for a management slot. He sucks up to the top brass, puts Galactic's balance sheet ahead of anything else, and still wants the crew to think of him as a brother. He's always sincere, no matter how little he means it."

That had been Seth's impression of the man in the one recorded glimpse he had obtained, but could he be so mean-spirited that he would leave two women to die out of personal dislike?

"When he pulled out, he posted a yellow flag, meaning plague. His beacon message dwelt on the hurricane-force winds and a virus that could penetrate all barriers. He never mentioned the centaurs at all."

"What? But I told him they were sentient! And I was right. Every time it rains or floods, they come visiting and leave fish offerings. That's *GenRegs' 196 [E]* behavior exactly. He should have posted a purple flag. Why yellow?"

"Perhaps to cover his ass for forbidding Tony Violaceus to try a rescue effort after you lost contact."

"Tony offered to do that? Jeez! He really is a great guy."

Seth thought he caught a faint afterthought of, "in bed, too," but that might be his own Old Adam grumbling. "Tony could have staked the planet for Galactic while he was at it. So perhaps Duddridge didn't want you rescued, babbling about talking otters? Your remarks from the shuttle can be dismissed as fevered delirium. He hoped to scare Mighty Mite out of sending down a shuttle, but he did not want to close the world to a later visit by Galactic. If this is the case, then he must think that there's some value in staking this planet. And you must have found it."

Meredith still worked for Galactic, not Mighty Mite. If she had found something valuable she might have told Duddridge and still want to keep it from Seth.

For a moment she said nothing. Then, "All we found was the centaurs, and they close down the whole planet. There's another thing, though. Doddery might have refused Tony's offer because he didn't want another death on his record. He lost people on both his previous missions, and now three more. Looks bad. You agree that the centaurs are sentient?"

Seth sighed. "After watching them bring you that fish just now because they understood that you were hungry and couldn't catch your own? You, a member of a species they had never met before? Of course I do. I think ISLA should put Cacafuego off-limits to development."

Scientific expeditions observing from space would be all. No explorers and no missionaries. What would missionaries preach to six-limbed natives anyway?

The shuttle's moves were becoming violent—erratic rises followed by sudden descents.

"Will Mighty Mite survive if it cannot stake the planet?"

"No. It will take ISLA years to decide whether to grant Mite a development permit or interdict Cacafuego and release the reward money. The reward won't even cover the interest on

Mite's debts." The publicity would help, of course, but not nearly enough. Seth's plog would be a bestseller, as would Meredith's, if she managed to pry the records out of Galactic. "We'll all be celebrities for a week or two." Especially JR. He'd love it. "And you can sue Galactic."

"Sue but never win."

"Oh, don't think that. They'll pay up millions to avoid the bad — *look out!*"

The shuttle shuddered as if it had been kicked. Then again. After a long tremor and a distant grating, tearing noise, it began to tilt.

Seth said, "Let's move to this side, just in..."

Too late. The cabin twisted violently and arranged the move for them. He slid, stopped with a jolt, and had all his breath knocked out by ninety kilos of Meredith running into him. Then they were buried under loose bedding. They had arrived on the original floor, although it still had a steep slope. Murky green daylight poured in through a window that had been hidden until now.

The movement didn't stop; it became a wild rocking. Clearly the front part of the shuttle had separated from the rest and was floating, basically right way up, but nose high. All that showed through the window was greenish water, with no surface or bottom in sight. He remembered that Galactic's second shuttle had disappeared, presumed washed out to sea — not a comforting thought.

"We must do this again in cozier surroundings," Meredith murmured.

"I guarantee full cooperation."

They disentangled as well as they could. Was their next trial to be seasickness? Roll, yaw, rock...

Seth said, "I'm sure *Golden Hind* is tracking us. The bow should be above water. I expect the tilt comes from all that sand in the lab. I don't think we'll go very far, and we're probably being swept inland. When the flood subsides, we'll run aground."

"A total lack of imagination is a good thing in a prospector."

"What are you imagining?"

"Don't ask."

Unfortunately, he didn't have to.

Their impromptu submarine continued its erratic motion, starting to spin as well as rock. It would meet no floating tree trunks, but it was moving so fast that any large rock could burst it open and sink it.

When humans couldn't play sex games or power games, they normally just chattered. So he chattered.

"Female prospectors are rare."

"Yes."

He waited.

"And most people called Meredith are herms? That what you're wondering?"

"But too polite to ask."

"I was named after my Uncle Auntie. My father was junior prospector on JKV's *Harmonious Chariot*. My mother was senior astrobiologist. They hit it off tops. They both wanted to make me a herm, but deep-space ships don't carry prenatal herm drugs. So here I am, permanently overwhelmed in the action."

"I don't mind underwhelming if you want a change. Born where?"

"On Earth. In Sweden."

"What happened to your parents?"

"Mother's still around, teaching at UNU. Father made the second descent to Blue Lantern."

"Um, quicksand, right?" It was a classic deep-space horror story. Twenty-odd years ago, so she could have no memory of him.

She nodded. "The first team landed on what looked like a beach beside a small lake and the shuttle sank in up its wings. With the jets plugged, it would have blown up if they had tried to take off. Then it started to move toward the pond. Nobody thought badly about that — quicksand is caused by underground artesian springs, so a slow flow down to the water seemed reasonable.

"Prospector Tsukuba brought the second shuttle down. He landed on the lake itself, as instructed. The plan was that he would throw ropes to the first crew, haul them off the beach, then fish them out of the water. He was standing on the wing of his shuttle, preparing to throw the first rope, when the shuttle was dragged under, and him with it. The whole thing, pond and beach, turned out to be a feeding orifice."

"I've seen the plog, what there was of it. All four people died."

"Blue Lantern was one of the bad ones, but we may match it. Ask me tomorrow."

"My immediate worry is getting seasick," Seth said.

They lay in silence for a while. He was physically exhausted, and had been running on his nerves for hours. Even so, he could not sleep in this blender.

Yet he must have dozed for a few minutes, because he was suddenly aware of Meredith tugging at her sheet.

"Right, Quasimodo." Her voice was slurred. "Pull out your rope and bells and start humping."

"Never met anyone as romantic as you, Juliet."

"I mean it, Stud." This was the stim shot speaking. "May be the last chance we'll ever have and I am hot to trot, ripe to rape, frantic to—"

"Not now! Wait until we're safely on *Golden Hind*, fed and clean and comfortable. Then I'll be at your service. All you can eat. These little piggies can go '*Oo! Oo! Oo!*' all the way home."

She muttered something inaudible. Her eyes stayed closed.

More light was coming in the window. Their submarine was rocking, pitching, and spinning even more violently in waves near the surface. Weeds were streaming past the glass. They looked like that ferny ground cover, so it was the shuttle that was moving at such an alarming rate, and the water wasn't very deep.

Then *thump!* The stern had grounded. Crunching noises. More violent thumps, felt in every bone he possessed. The light brightened.

"That's good," he said. "We're surfacing."

No answer.

Four smaller bumps and a big one and all motion stopped.

The water level sank steadily down the glass.

Seth swallowed his heart back where it belonged. "Please remain seated with your safety web fastened until the shuttle has come to a complete stop at the terminal building."

The cabin was resting on its belly, almost level. The door that had been in the ceiling was now at the far side of the room, easily accessible.

He waited to make sure that there were no more surprises coming but his eyelids started drooping, so he sat up. Having made sure Meredith was comfortable and not likely to choke, he rose to peer out the window. All he could see was rain and an extremely rough wall, reminiscent of a coral reef, decorated with "moss" and "barnacles". He could guess what that was.

He might be going to survive this crazy adventure after all.

He dug through the litter to find his headband, then walked up the slant of the deck to the corridor door. And hesitated. The corridor might be full of water. There had been two dead bodies in the shuttle before it broke apart. He did not know their present whereabouts, and they would be in loathsome condition after three weeks of unrelenting heat. The door opened easily to his touch. He detected no foul stench of death.

The window on that side showed another chimney about two meters away, half hidden in driving rain. He could hear nothing except the noise of the storm, although that seemed to be slackening. If the centaurs had any sense, they were staying indoors. The corridor, like *Niagara*'s, was divided by airtight doors. The first one aft was warped and immovable, but there was probably nothing left beyond it anyway. If he couldn't get out, centaurs could not get in.

Forward the corridor brought him to the starboard exit door. He decided not to try it, because if he couldn't open it, he probably couldn't get out at all. He would cross that bridge when he got to it.

Now the passage ended at a door that he guessed would lead to the prospectors' quarters. Normally only Control could open bulkhead doors, but with the power off all he need do was tug on the emergency lever. Inside, he found no bodies, just a dormitory for two, a toilet, and the door to the cab. The heat was terrible, the air stale and nasty. Rummaging in cupboards, he found the most welcome sight of his life, a crate of water bottles. He gulped a quarter of a bottle without drawing breath.

His search found no bodies and ended in the cab itself. In the absence of power, the view screens had all reverted to windows, and he was able to look out at the chimney colony. There were still no centaurs in sight, but visibility was restricted by rain. Aft, past where the shuttle's wing had been, he could glimpse a spread of flat sand, broad enough for *Niagara* to land on, and that was a very welcome sight.

Armed with a second water bottle, he settled into the master's chair. The glass should not block transmission as the metal hull had.

"Prospector to *Golden Hind*."

At least three voices yelled, "Seth!" simultaneously. The ship must be passing almost directly overhead, for he detected no delay.

"Meredith and I are both alive, in the forward end of the shuttle, jammed in the chimney forest."

Jordan: "Yes, we can see it. The other half didn't go far, but if you'd been a hundred meters farther north, you'd have gone straight past and out to sea."

"Must be the gods' reward for virtuous living. How's the weather look?" He was resigned to hearing that another week ought to do it.

"It looks good for about four hours from now, but our orbit isn't properly lined up. We can jump if it's urgent, but there's a big tropical high due in about eight hours. That should give you some relatively calm weather. And you must need some sleep."

He'd believe in calm on this violent planet when he saw it. "Is my plog uploading?"

"Control says it's all done."

"Good. There is a problem. Meredith is unconscious. I haven't tried to waken her, but I think she's in coma. It's probably a reaction to the stim shot, on top of narcosis, dehydration, and a diet of raw fish. Emotional trauma too, I expect. Dare I give her another stim shot before the shuttle lands? I can't carry her in this gravity."

Pause for murmured consultation...

"Seth? Jordan again. Control and Reese both say no, don't risk it. We'll try to concoct something safer for her and send it down with the shuttle. How close can it land?"

"The closer the better as far as I'm concerned. It seems flat enough behind the cab, but it's raining too hard to be sure. Don't argue with the chimneys, they're natural formations, solid rock."

"We won't."

"Come down on sand if you can. Both of us will need depressurizing, especially Meredith, and we should both be quarantined, because I had to break asepsis."

"We're working on that assumption."

Seth drew a deep breath. "I want to go on record as agreeing with Meredith Tsukuba's opinion that the centaurs are sentient." He heard JC utter his favorite oath in the background. "They were bringing offerings of fish to her. They carry weapons and gourds. They don't harm us as long as we aren't wearing clothes. They have complex calls that seem to be language."

He had wanted fortune and must settle for fame.

"Control has analyzed your earlier plog," Jordan's voice said, "and agrees with you on the language."

"They don't build the chimneys, but they nest in them, so they're around here somewhere. Toss some clothes into the shuttle for both of us, please. We'll have to strip naked to get to it."

"Your plog ought to be Top of the Pops."

"Only if it has a happy ending. I must sign off now and get some rest. I haven't slept in years."

He checked on Meredith. She was still asleep, her pulse worrisomely faint. He went back to the prospectors' dormitory and, with a huge sigh of relief, sank down on the lower bunk, which was probably hers. He was asleep before his eyes closed.

DAY 414

001.102 POTENTIAL CARRIER means a person who has been exposed to an exoplanetary atmosphere, or has in any way whatsoever come into contact with alien life forms, whether visible or microscopic, known or suspected, or who has had any opportunity whatsoever of having been contaminated, directly or indirectly, by alien life forms, known or suspected.

029.07 Potential Carriers shall be quarantined in an approved facility for the greatest of:

[a] Forty days after the possible exposure or
      contamination,

[b] Forty days after all signs of infection or disease
      have disappeared,

[c] As long as the responsible medical authority
      may order.

General Regulations
InterStellar Licensing Authority
2375 edition

⊶═◉   ✴   ◉═⊷

Seth was wakened by nothing more deadly or exotic than a full bladder. Nothing less would have done so. For a few moments he was lost and bewildered, wondering where he was, why he ached all over, why he was so hungry. He heaved himself out of bed and went to the toilet.

He checked on Meredith, who was still breathing, but unresponsive. Without prompt medical aid she might never waken.

He went back to the cabin and studied the view for a moment. The sun was low, the sky pale blue and cloudless. On both sides and straight ahead the windows looked out on a forest of chimneys, as tall as three-story houses, but rough, irregular, mostly lopsided. At close quarters they were obviously natural, not at all artificial. Looking aft through the starboard ports, he could just make out a featureless plain of rounded boulders and cobbles. The ferny groundcover was barely moving. There was a dry sandy patch not far off.

"Prospector to *Golden Hind*."

After a brief delay for relaying, Hanna's voice answered. "We read you, Seth."

"What news?"

"*Niagara*'s on its way. Your pizza will be delivered in about an hour."

"I won't say no to that. Weather couldn't be better. About a hundred meters west looks dead flat. I'd better go out and take a look. I'll call... Can you see what I see?"

Centaurs were emerging from the chimneys, scrambling down the sides backwards. Those claws had more uses than just catching fish. There were dozens of the critters — scores, more than a hundred. He couldn't hear through the glass, but he could tell by their movements that they were excited and jabbering. It seemed odd that they had not noticed the remains of *Mercury* on their doorstep before now. Then he realized that they were gathering under his window to stare up at him. It was not the shuttle that had excited them, it was its occupant. Mothers were pointing him out to their babies.

"They're so *cute!*" Hanna said. "They look like little medieval war horses caparisoned for jousting."

Horses did not have pointed teeth like these critters. On impulse, Seth waved. Instantly fifty or sixty flippers waved back at him, each little "arm" flapping a black-and-white flag. He waved both hands. They copied him again, and he had a strange feeling that they were laughing. *Monkey see, monkey do.*

"I'm going out to inspect the landing site," he said. "I daren't take my com or my video with me. Prospector out." He cut off Hanna's squawk of alarm.

He had no shoes. Back in the prospectors' dormitory he found a heap of clothes on the topmost bunk. A glance at the shirt showed that they had belonged to the late Dylan Guinizelli, whom

Meredith had called a big man. Big, as in huge. Here Dylan had stripped down to put on his EVA suit, but he had been treated in the infirmary and never returned for them. Seth could see no footwear, but the dead prospector's shoes would not have fitted him anyway. He had reached the exterior door before he realized that the door opened downward, to double as a ladder.

"Prospector to *Golden Hind*. Disregard previous message. Planned EVA is cancelled. The shuttle has no power, so I won't be able to close the darned thing once I open it." Centaurs were nimble climbers.

"Which is what I was trying to tell you, you muscle-bound bonehead!"

From Hanna, that was gutter talk. He was amused.

"If I wasn't what you just called me, I wouldn't be here, now would I? How long is the weather window?"

"Three hours or more. Not counting clear air turbulence, of course. You should have plenty of time."

"Meredith's in a coma. I'll try to carry her, but it won't be easy and it won't be quick." If the centaurs got in his way, it would probably be impossible.

"I'll be praying for both of you, Seth."

"Good thinking. Prospector out."

Hoping to find something to eat other than Meredith's raw fish, which would be putrid by now, he hunted through the prospectors' supplies. He had no success. Anything edible would have been kept in the galley.

The centaurs were still all around the shuttle, waiting for more glimpses of the alien. Whenever he approached a window, the watchers outside would shout and wave, and others would come running. He decided it would be a good idea to let them grow accustomed to seeing him with his headband on. Maybe then they would let him leave with it. His plog was safely archived on *Golden Hind*, but he wanted to record his departure.

"*Golden Hind* to Prospector." Hanna again.

"I copy you."

"*Niagara* will be landing in five minutes."

He was astonished to feel a sudden lump in his throat. Was the ordeal almost over? His great adventure, the aim of his life, the day for which he would be forever remembered? Nearly finished?

"Maybe this time I'll accept a few prayers, then. Meredith is still in coma. Can I give her a stim shot?"

There was a moment's pause and the next voice belonged to Reese, who doubled as medical director.

"Under normal circumstances, no medical protocol would allow it. However, if that is her only hope of survival, then you'll have to risk it. Leave your camera in another room when you do."

"Thanks a bundle. Prospector out."

The shuttle must come in from the west and he had no clear view in that direction, but he could watch the centaurs outside. Damn, but they were cute! He waved, they waved. He managed a clumsy little dance. They danced. He noticed that there were always a few clambering up or down the sides of chimneys; with their middle and rear limbs spread out they looked like giant bats. Meredith had suggested that their hairless skin dried out in the sunshine and they liked to stay damp. Whatever creatures made the chimneys always grew near a river mouth or the sea.

He went back to check on Meredith and found her condition unchanged. How was he going to transport her if he couldn't carry her? The simplest way would be to strap her on a stretcher and drag one end, trailing the other like a travois. No doubt this flying palace had included a stretcher in its medical supplies, but it would not likely have been stored in the bow section. He had not found one, and could think of no way to improvise one. He attacked one of the bunks with his bare hands, hoping he could somehow detach the frame, but he made no impression at all. The mattresses were too flexible. The nearest he found to anything useful was a metal rod from a closet. He needed two of them, each twice as long.

The waiting was getting to him. He had a headache.

He returned to the cab, where the larger windows gave the best view of the landing ground. The centaurs were all facing west, hearing something.

The dream is over. Ready to wake up and go back to waiting on tables, Master?

The centaurs stampeded, fleeing to the safety of the chimneys, which probably meant underwater. The chimneys were always wet, always seeping. So when winter brought snow instead of rain, they would drain completely and their porous walls would provide insulation, while their exteriors would be sealed by ice. Storm surges would pile sea ice around them, natural igloos with rocky cores. It was quite possible that the centaurs could hibernate inside them.

A shadow passed slowly overhead. *Niagara* blew fire on the sand, then settled in a perfect landing. Seth released his breath with a rush, not having realized that he had been holding it. He passed on the good news to the ship, although Control would be monitoring and reporting.

"Seth," Jordan said, "Control doesn't give much for Meredith's chances of surviving, even if you can deliver her safely to *Golden Hind*. I know you'll do your best to save her, but don't kill yourself trying. That's an order, Prospector."

Seth said, "Yes, sir." They both knew that no one could give him orders while he was master of *Niagara*, but the captain might feel better for having tried.

His headache was worse. He was shivering, despite the heat. Whatever had infected the Galactic crew was getting to him too. That was another reason not to waste time.

The shuttle's skin would be cool by the time he reached it, if he ever did. He went back to Meredith. She was still alive, barely. Again he tried to lift her, but she was completely limp and here she weighed more than he would back on Earth. He would have to negotiate the ladder down to the ground, drag her over some nasty terrain, and arrive at *Niagara* with enough strength to carry her up the ladder there. If he dropped her, he might kill her.

He couldn't do it.

Damn!

Think...

He laid his precious sample bag nearby and closed all the doors except the one to Meredith's sickroom. Then he armed himself with the curtain rod, went to the exit, unfastened the manual clamps, and let the door fall open. The fuselage was too close to the ground, so it dropped to about a forty-five degree angle, instead of all the way to vertical.

A few centaurs had emerged and gone to inspect *Niagara* from what they must think was a safe distance, yittering nervously about the traces of steam still rising from the sand. Their panda-like faces swung around when Seth appeared in *Mercury*'s doorway. He beckoned them.

They came running, caparisons flapping. They gathered around the ladder. Fortunately, there was a spear-carrier among them. Seth must gamble that the spears were a symbol of rank. He pointed his curtain rod at that one and beckoned with his free hand.

Much yittering.

"Come here, dammit! You think I can stand for hours in this damnable gravity, waiting for you? Yes, you. Come here!"

The spear-carrier understood the gestures, if not the words, and advanced to the foot of the ladder, others clearing a path for him, or perhaps her — unless they were carrying young, they were as hard to sex as penguins. Seth stepped aside and beckoned for it to enter.

The spear-carrier scurried up the ramp at once, nosey as a monkey. Seth led the way to Meredith.

The centaur uttered what sounded like an alarm cry. It... he ... poked her arm with a flipper, stroked her hair, made a strange noise that sounded mostly like a chuckle but could well be a Cacafuegian distress call.

"I need help, you cute little idiot. Summon your friends and relations. I want you to carry her for me. Like this." Seth tugged the edge of the sheet, to show how that worked. Then he cradled the sample bag in his arms like a baby. "So jump on all six feet, understand?" He pointed an arm in *Niagara*'s direction, cradled the bag again.

Seth had found the Albert Einstein of Cacafuego: the apple dropped, understanding dawned. The centaur rushed out into the corridor, where several others had arrived.

Yitter yitter yitter yitter yitter...

One thing they had in common with humans was that they never stopped talking.

But his desperate plan worked. About eight of them crowded into the dormitory. They all kept yittering, but Einstein yittered loudest. Under his direction, they hoisted Meredith shoulder high — their shoulders — which were about thigh-height on Seth. He led the way, down the ramp, and off toward *Niagara*, aware that Control would be recording this procession and wondering how it was going to play on his plog: history being made, a naked human conscripting a team of hexapod aliens to carry another human to safety. Or perhaps to a barbecue pit? He held the sample bag before him in a strategic location, partly for modesty, but also to protect important locations from the centaur's busily exploring flippers. They found his legs fascinating.

He dared not stop to rest and he was staggering by the time he reached the shuttle. The door swung down for him, alarming his escort just enough that he managed to be first up the ramp. The two-meter climb was almost beyond his strength.

Overhead, the first bulkhead hatch of the Gut was closed, restricting the entrance to what would normally be the decontamination chamber. The rest of the shuttle would not be infested by centaurs, which might see *Niagara* as a giant chimney and want to explore it.

There was little enough room for Meredith as well, but Einstein yittered orders, many eager flippers raised her, and Seth somehow managed to haul her in, at the risk of wrecking his back. He arranged her, sitting against the wall, knees up. Then he gently resisted efforts for the whole tribe to join him. One of them was a spear-carrier — probably Einstein, although he still could not tell one Cacafuegian from another. Seth offered to trade a priceless imported curtain rod for a wooden spear armed with a sharp shell point. Einstein caught on at once and yittered loudly as they made the exchange.

ISLA would throw purple fits, of course, but if the centaurs were not already rummaging all through what remained of *Mercury*, they wouldn't need long to work out how the doors opened. They would find bedding, clothes, and many other goodies. Seth had broken every rule in *GenRegs 002*, the section that dealt with first contact, and would face a charge sheet as long as his arm. He would plead *force majeure* and sanctity of human life. More important, he was going to be an international hero, so ISLA wouldn't dare penalize him harshly. Just fine him a million dollars or so. By then he wouldn't care about small change like that.

"Control, start raising the ramp, but go slowly until the centaurs are all off it."

The centaurs quickly took the hint, with Einstein scrambling to safety behind his followers. Control slammed the door. Seth sat down beside Meredith, which was a tight fit. He was starting to see double and his head felt like it was about to burst.

"Seth, this is Jordan. You read me?"

"I copy," he mumbled.

"You can't survive takeoff in that position."

"We'll have to. I can't climb the ladder myself, let alone do it for two. Wake me when ... in orbit. And don't," he muttered, "let Control fumigate us with toxic chemicals. Prospector ... out."

DAYS 415-422

002.002 Sampling is forbidden on any world on which a Sentience Alert Beacon has been posted. As soon as a possibly sentient species is encountered, all materials, living or dead, previously or subsequently gathered on that world, automatically become the property of ISLA.

General Regulations
InterStellar Licensing Authority
2375 edition

⊷═◉ ✷ ◉═⊶

Seth had no recollection at all of the next two days, and only spotty memories of the two after that. He gradually became aware that he was aboard *Niagara*, lying in the prospector's bunk. Once in a while, someone would come to fuss over him, instead of just leaving him to die in peace as he wanted. When, at last, he could force his eyes to focus, he determined that his tormentor was Reese Platte, still female, and wearing an aseptic suit. She was doing something with heavy web straps.

"Oh, you're back?" she said cheerily. "How do you feel?"

"*Groan.*"

"Well, that's better than nothing, and much better than all the things you've been saying lately."

"Uh?"

"Doesn't matter. Just delirium. Can't be held against you. We had to strap you down. You're not going to erupt again, are you? Convulsions in free fall are not as dangerous as they are in gravity, but you might still damage yourself. I am going to give you a sponge bath. Yes, I certainly am, because at the moment you would qualify as toxic waste under the Oslo Convention."

→⊨● ✸ ●=⊨←

He came to his senses fairly rapidly in the hours after that, although physically he was as weak as a newborn. His next visitor was Hanna, wearing ordinary ship gear. She had come to remove his IV feed and give him a bulb of pseudo-chicken soup.

He felt strong enough to ask. "I take it that I am no longer in quarantine?"

"No." That answer was suspiciously lacking in detail.

"I can rejoin the party, then?"

"Not yet. We're still depressurizing Meredith, and you have to stay in the shuttle with her unless you want to risk an attack of the bends yourself."

"How is she?"

"She's recovering. She had a dozen rampant infections and parasites — all of which we dealt with — but mostly she was suffering from major nitrogen narcosis. No signs of anything unknown, and Control says she'll live."

"And me?"

"Unknown pathogen, but you're recovering too."

"Where are we going? Home or Armada?

"Home. We decided that as soon as *Niagara* left Cacafuego. Our life systems will be too close to critical when they must support seven people. Also we're out of shuttle fuel."

Seth decided he would go and see Meredith as soon as Hanna left. Instead, he fell asleep.

He learned later that he had not been as helpless as he thought. As soon as the shuttle had reached orbit, he had reacted as if he were conscious. He had floated Meredith along the Gut and strapped her down in the biologist's bunk, then attached three pressure-driven intravenous feeds, which had been left there in readiness for her. He had even stowed his sample bag in the lab freezer before putting himself to bed, but he had no memory of doing any of those things. Control had docked the shuttle, and Reese had boarded to tend the invalids.

His next visitor was the captain herself, bringing more food and looking haggard. Seth accepted the bag but left it floating within easy reach.

"Tell me."

"Tell you what?"

136

"Your troubles. You can't fool me. Speak up." Why, for instance, had they decided to change over so soon? Usually they stayed one gender for at least a month.

Jordan smiled ruefully and folded into a sitting posture. "I was planning a special welcome-home ceremony, but I discovered I'd have to restrain myself for a few days. Eat up. You can help best by getting your strength back. We think we can risk returning you to standard atmospheric pressure in three or four days."

"So you're shorthanded. Where's Reese?"

"In bed. And JC also. 'Unknown pathogen.' Meredith was right when she said this thing could escape any containment."

"But what is it?" A century of galactic exploration had turned up a fantastic variety of viruses and bacteria. It seemed incredible that there could be anything really new to human medical science now. Reese and Control between them should be able to type any sort of infective agent and zap it with the appropriate drugs.

"They don't know. Meredith survived it and it looks as if you will. The rest of us can only hope we'll do as well when we catch it. Drink your soup while it's hot."

"Next time bring a steak."

"Soft biscuits and warm milk."

Seth said something no gentleman should say to a lady.

When Jordan had hurried off to attend to a million duties, Seth drank soup and brooded over the news. In theory the trip back to Earth should take only a few days, retracing the jumps they had made on the way here. In practice, space was never still, and *Golden Hind* had journeyed not merely 1,500 light years' distance, but at least 1,500 years. If one of their havens had disappeared, Hanna would have to start all over, ferreting out a new route.

When *Golden Hind* arrived in near-Earth space, Control would automatically report this unknown infection and ISLA would slap a quarantine order on the ship. There were very few precedents for that, and no way of knowing how long the ban would last. Of course the news of a sentient species would ring around the world, but the new celebrities would not be available to be feted.

Seth was a made man. He would have his plog edited into shape by then and royalties would come pouring in for years. Meredith might work up hers from Galactic's records, but it would not be as complete or as dramatic as Seth's. She would have a cast-iron legal case against Galactic for attempted murder, so in the end she would be rich also.

But the others? They would be famous and broke. *Golden Hind* would be seized by the banks and the crew would be very lucky to see even the termination bonuses they had been promised in their contracts. They would not benefit from the samples Seth had so diligently collected. Even if everyone recovered completely from the mysterious infection, the voyage home was not going to be a happy one.

After eating, he decided to pay a call on his fellow sufferer. Wrapping himself in a bed sheet — since no one had yet thought to bring him any clothes — he floated along the Gut to the biologist's cabin to visit with Meredith. Even in free fall, he felt weak, tending to bounce off walls. He found her alert, reading text on the monitor, and wearing very little more than he was. She was barely recognizable as the bedraggled, starving, poisoned, wreck he had known on the planet. Now she was a dream of womankind, her hair clean and shiny, her eyes bright. The way they lit up at the sight of him was flattering.

"How are you feeling?" he asked.

"Great, thanks to you. I've watched dozens of replays of me being carried by that team of stretcher-bearers you organized. It's incredible! However did you do it?"

"Out of desperation. They're smart little critters."

"Well I can't thank them, but I am eternally grateful to you."

"No need. I'd have done it for anyone, even JC. It wasn't just because you're a red-hot sex bomb."

"I bet that helped." Golden eyebrows rose.

"You bet," he admitted.

"So you do hope to cash in your IOU's some time?"

His denial died stillborn. He nodded.

She said, "There is never any time like the present."

Testosterone receptors started flashing in Seth's limbic area. "I'm still as weak as a newborn kitten."

"I can fix that."

He floated a little closer. "Sounds dangerous. I ought to get into shape first."

"We must begin your training at once."

He had to kiss her then. Her response was anything but sisterly, and for the next thirty minutes or so conversation was brief and incoherent.

Golden Hind's shuttle had always been off-limits to everyone except the prospector, but Seth had invited Jordan up there a couple of times "for an inspection." The inspections had been mutual and intimate. So he'd had experience in free fall sex and knew how it was done. If Meredith did not, she had a natural gift for it. Convalescence was going to be a lot less boring from now on. As they floated in recovery mode, still tightly entwined, he reflected that this had been the fastest wooing he'd ever heard of.

"Mm," she murmured. "That was very nice. What's your turnaround time?"

"Usually an hour or so, but after that epic, I feel like I'll need a month."

"Dylan used to manage a lap every twenty minutes."

"Screw Dylan."

"I did. I bet I can bring you up to speed too."

"You have my permission to try."

Meredith was not only an enthusiast, she was an expert. She came close–twenty-seven minutes.

Paradise was short-lived though. Two days later, Control reported that the convalescents should now be able to return to standard atmospheric pressure, and they both reported for duty. Everyone else except Jordan had succumbed to the mysterious plague. Reese had been first to go and ought to be first to recover. *Golden Hind* was drifting in a haven about two hundred light years from Cacafuego. So far Hanna had been able to retrace the incoming jumps, but no one was willing to step into her shoes as navigator. A few days' delay hardly mattered on such a journey.

By evening, Jordan looked blurred and battered; she reluctantly admitted to having a headache, which was the first sign of the mysterious infection. Seth fetched the medic tester. As soon as it took a blood sample, Control ordered complete bed rest. Jordan gratefully staggered off in search of an empty bunk. Was Seth Broderick now in charge?

In the commodore's stateroom, Reese was conscious, but apparently content to lie and stare at the ceiling. Tied down on the other bed like a beached whale, JC mumbled and twitched in delirium.

"Dr. Platte, ma'am, I have the honor of informing you that you are now the ranking officer aboard. Ma'am?"

Reese rolled her eyes in his direction without moving her head. While she did not look her legal age of ninety-four, she was certainly not at her best. Her hair was a limp tangle; the clumsy tuck in her lip was more evident than usual.

"What do you expect me to do?"

"Take charge, ma'am."

"I'm not capable at the moment. You, on the other hand, are Mr. Know-it-all, the universal understudy for the entire crew. Consider yourself acting captain until further notice."

Seth felt as if he needed to shake seawater out of his ears. Since when had Reese ever paid anyone a compliment, especially him?

"Is that an order, ma'am?"

"No, it's a statement of fact. You are the most fucking infuriating asshole, Broderick. You could run this ship singlehanded. You always know best. You run up the wildest prospector's plog in history, which will bring you billions. You discover the only other intelligent species in the galaxy, so the rest of us will get nothing. Giving you orders doesn't do any good. You don't even take direct orders from the captain. I'd report you for mutiny if I wasn't so ashamed."

Seth's scalp prickled. Either Reese was still delirious or she had suffered serious brain damage.

"Just when did I refuse a direct order from the captain?"

"When he ordered you to rape me."

"Ma'am, one of us is having delusions. Captain Spears never did that, and never would."

"They told me they did."

Those bizarre hints… "You actually *asked* Jordan to tell me to do that?"

"Of course. I begged him to. He said he had, pretty much. But you didn't do it. You think I'm old and ugly, don't you?"

Before he could bite his tongue off, Seth said, "Pretty much. I mean you don't look so hot right now."

"When did I ever look hot to you?"

Seth jumped for the door. He slammed it behind him and stood out for a few minutes in the corridor, shaking and sweating. Eventually he whispered, "Fucking never." After that he felt better.

→⇒◉ ✷ ◉⇐←

He went back to the control room, where a weary-looking Meredith was fixedly watching a line of camels parading along the aft wall. Seth spread both hands on the table, and appointed himself acting captain. With surprising little difficulty, he persuaded Control to recognize Meredith as his deputy.

"I'd rather be first mate," she said.

"No, that was my singing teacher, ten years ago."

"She must have been a real prima donna."

"She was good on encores, although not in your class. Why don't you go off and get some sleep? There's one bed left in the middle cabin. I know GenRegs insists that a human be awake at all times, but this is an emergency, so we can overrule it. I'll make myself comfortable in the mess."

Meredith stood up and reached out a hand to him. "Why don't we both mess around in the mess first?"

A gentleman never refused a lady, especially that one.

⊷⊷⊨⊚ ✶ ⊚⊨⊷⊶

Apart from the hydroponics, which needed a few hours' attention every week, the ship almost ran itself. That was fortunate, because the acting captain and his deputy were kept busy attending to the invalids. Age seemed to make a difference. Both JC and Reese took a long time to recover. Hanna bounced back surprisingly quickly and was the first to venture as far as the mess.

Seth found her there drinking coffee when he returned from giving the semi-conscious JC a sponge bath. Her gorgeous red-gold hair had recovered its shine and her smile was not far behind. Of course, anyone would look good after JC.

"You look much better!" he said.

"And you look as gorgeous as always." She turned scarlet. "I didn't mean to say that!"

"Please don't let my natural modesty stop you if you have anything more to add along the same lines." He headed for the coffee.

Hanna wrapped her hands around her cup and stared down at it, not meeting his eye. "I am deeply ashamed of the way I've treated you, Seth. I've always tried to live by the principles my parents... I mean... No, let me say my piece. I was brought up to believe certain things and have always abided by them and I have never had cause to question them, but I see now that this is no longer the world for which those rules were ... I mean they don't necessarily apply as strongly in today's society when we have ... like, medical advances, for one thing. And we have unmarried men and women shut up together in close proximity for very long times, and I understand that men, especially young men, have stronger needs than women do and I deeply appreciate that you never questioned my decision or argued, unlike some others I could mention, and I respect you very much for that and I respect you even more for that wonderful EVA you just completed and the way you rescued that Tsukuba bitch, and if you and I find ourselves sharing a cabin again on the way home, I will let you … I mean I will try to be more cooperative and understanding."

Good God! Had the entire crew gone insane?

This was where Seth must say that he completely understood her feelings and respected her beliefs, and that he would on no account expect her to deviate from her principles for his sake.

The words stuck in his throat. He could not be such a hypocrite, after all the times he had lain in the dark and cursed her. The right answer would be something like, "Right on!" but he managed to keep it to a mumbled, "Thank you. I look forward very much to accepting your offer at the earliest possible—"

Face as red as her hair, Hanna jumped up and ran out of the room.

⊷═◉ 🟊 ◉═⊶

The day after that, she declared herself fit for duty and assumed command. She set to work planning the next jump, leaving Seth and Meredith to continue their hospital duties. Two days later, Jordan and Reese returned to work also. Only JC was still too weak to climb out of bed.

Seth ran into Jordan in the showers. He was shaving; she had been showering and emerged rubbing her hair with a towel. Eyes met in the mirror. Icicles formed amid the steam.

"Good to see you operational again, ma'am."

"And you're quite back to your old self, aren't you?"

Seth examined his upper lip carefully, but decided that there was no escape from words like that spoken like that. "What do you mean?"

"Meredith Tsukuba's a good lay, is she?"

Denying it would be futile. Crew behavior was the captain's prime responsibility, so while Control would not gossip to other people, it would not refuse a direct question from the captain. Besides, women always knew such things by instinct. Although Seth had proposed marriage to Jordan, since then he and Meredith had been humping like alley cats. They might have been reacting to a harrowing shared adventure, or just indulging in rampant lechery. No matter; he was doomed whatever he said now. He shrugged.

"She's really good — eager, inventive… Try her, next time you switch."

142

He stared at his reflection. There was no cartoon icon above his head to indicate a flash of inspiration. But there should be! And like all great ideas it provoked a why-did-I-not-see-this-sooner? reaction. Blind idiot!

Meanwhile he had missed what the captain had said.

"Beg pardon, ma'am?"

"I said I have to reassign cabins. We'll need to hot-bunk some."

"I could fetch bedding from the shuttle, doss down in the elevator. Should be warm enough if we leave the door open."

"We can do better than that." The captain stalked over to the door.

Seth said softly. "Jordie?"

She looked back, eyes cold.

He said, "My offer is still open."

"No, it isn't." She reached for the door handle.

"Wait!" Seth called. "We haven't had the wake yet."

The wake was a spacer tradition, an all-hands, no-holds-barred review held on quitting a world, when everyone concerned could report, brag, or complain. It could be a funeral or a celebration, or both.

Jordan's glare informed Seth that it was the captain who called the wake. "I'm waiting until the commodore could join us."

"I think it should be held as soon as possible, ma'am. Very urgent."

"Why?"

"I believe it would be advantageous for, um, most of us."

At that moment Reese came in. She glanced from one to the other and read the body language. "This a private fight, or can anyone join in?"

"Take a number." Seth turned back to the mirror — where he saw both women blush.

Jordan said, "How's JC, Reese? Could he attend a wake this afternoon?"

DAY 423

I've told you about Blackadder's Law: "Every world is different, except that they're all out to get you." Once in a while, though, a wildcatter will smile and whisper what is known, for obvious reasons, as "Whiteadder's Amendment." Its wording varies widely, but is usually along the lines of, "But sometimes one will give you a very special treat."

Fonatelles, op. cit.

⇥ ✷ ⇤

The walls and ceiling of the control room were displaying the starscape outside, dominated by the devilish red glow of great Betelgeuse, although the blue giant Bellatrix now glowed significantly brighter than before. Seth had brought a chair from the mess for Meredith and placed it beside his own at the foot of the table. She was in it already, stroking Whittington, while that faithless turncoat purred in her lap. One by one the others drifted in: Reese, annoyed to be dragged away from the lab, where she had been studying Cacafuego fever; Hanna fidgeting because one of her ferrets was late returning; Jordan still pale from her sickness; and Maria, who honored Seth with a sultry smile designed to boost his heart beat significantly, deliberately followed by a stare at Meredith intended to stop hers altogether. There were now two sex bombs aboard *Golden Hind*, an explosive mixture even without including Seth's earlier commitment to the captain.

Lastly came JC, grayer and significantly thinner after his ordeal. He was not so reduced that he could not play the royal role, though. He smiled graciously to his loyal subjects and took the chair at the head of the table, normally occupied by the captain. That was another part of the tradition, for a wake had no fixed agenda, and even the captain's performance could be shredded. The record was invariably submitted as a report to the financial backers and almost always made public too, so that reputations could be made or shattered. In a wake the ambitious could try to boost their careers and the spiteful could satisfy grudges. Wakes had been known to end in brawls and attempted murder.

Seth savored nostalgic memories of other meetings around this table: jubilation at the announcement that they were heading to a niner world, joy when they saw it for the first time, dismay when they found the beacon, and the dawning hope later that there might yet be something to salvage. Now the mood was sour, almost putrid. It was not the planet at fault now, it was the people. The team had lost faith in itself. He thought he knew why, and was astonished that no one else seemed to have worked it out.

JC had barely laid his hand on the table when he was interrupted by a rainbow flash outside the ship — the missing ferret had returned from a jump. Hanna half rose, then settled back. Control could dock the probe and download its information. An hour or two didn't matter.

"A good omen!" JC said. "Control, the wake is in session. Lights, please."

The universe disappeared, beige walls and ceiling returned. Something of the old JC was revealed also. He knew all there was to know about chairing meetings. When it came to public relations, he could spin like a pulsar. Leaning back, relaxed in his chair, he beamed around and addressed Posterity.

"It is a great honor to preside at this historic wake aboard Mighty Mite's Deep Space Ship *Golden Hind*, presently wending its way homeward after its epic visit to the world we have named Cacafuego, ISLA catalogue number GK79986B. Before summarizing the team's astonishing discoveries, I must pay credit…" To Jordan for a harmonious voyage out, to Hanna for a speedy and safe one, to Maria for a skilled analysis of the problem world…

"And certainly to the renowned Dr. Reese Platte, our biologist, who has not merely nursed every one of us back to health in her capacity as chief medical officer, but has managed to solve the mystery of the unknown infection that—"

Jordan's fist hit the table. "Just when does Dr. Platte plan to share her findings with the rest of us?" Her expression made quite clear that she had not been told the news beforehand. For Reese to tip off JC before telling the captain was a serious discourtesy at the very least.

"I was planning to start personal statements after—"

"Now!" Jordan barked. "Or I will suspend this wake until First Officer Finn and I have been properly briefed." She wasn't having any trouble standing up to Commodore Lecanard now, but perhaps that was because it was Reese she was really mad at. Or else JC looked less formidable than before.

"I truly meant no disrespect, ma'am," Reese said, and for once she seemed defensive, not smirking or sneering. "So far my findings are provisional, but when I went to check on the commodore this morning, he did ask me if I had identified the infective agent yet and I let slip that I had."

Of course!

"You have a name for it?"

"Not yet, ma'am. I am not ready to submit a detailed report, but I am convinced now that the culprit is a prion."

"A what?"

"A prion. A prion is a protein of the same chemical composition as one of the victim's own constituent proteins, but wrongly folded. Infective prions were discovered back in the twentieth century, but they are so rare that I have discovered few later references in Control's library. They are associated with disease of the brain, specifically *spongiform encephalopathy*, where the brain is reduced to a sponge. They are normally spread by eating infected brain tissue, although in this case by some other means, most likely simple inhalation. As a first hypothesis, the prion protein we contracted may have come from the centaurs. Perhaps it is peculiarly associated with intelligence? Notably the first to succumb was Prospector Dylan Guinizelli. He was swarmed by them, as you will recall."

"His EVA suit was not compromised!" Meredith said. "I insist on that."

Reese shot her a glance of dislike. "You cannot know that. A prion is so tiny, far smaller even than a virus particle, that it could have penetrated any mechanical junction, such as the seal of his helmet. Even if it just adhered to the outside of his suit, your later attempts at decontamination would have been useless. Known prions are so stable that they will survive being boiled in caustic soda.

"The danger is that when a prion meets up with its normal twin, it catalyzes the normal protein's inversion into the evil twin's own form. Thus it creates a stereo copy of itself, and both can then proceed to catalyze others."

"Like vampires?" Maria muttered.

"Or nuclear chain reactions," JC said.

No one else commented. All eyes were fixed on Reese, hanging on her words.

"And what is the cure?" Jordan asked.

"No cure is known," Reese said. She smiled smugly. "No one ever survives a prion infection. I detected no trace of antibodies being formed against the infection, because the intruder is identical or almost identical to one of our own constituents. Our immune system ignores it. But since we here are all either cured or recovering, I knew at once that there must be a treatment in this case. We have been incredibly lucky. Had I not been summoned to this wake, I would be in my lab continuing my research. I guessed that the answer must lie in one of the medications we have been using. Since viruses have protein coats, I began by trying out the standard intravenous antiviral medications that ISLA recommends, and about ten minutes ago I found that the evil-twin prions in one of my Petri dishes were reverting to their regular form. Serendipitously, the antidote lay in that medication, and now all I have to do is isolate which ingredient is the active agent."

"Brilliant!" Jordan jumped to her feet and applauded, and everyone else followed, although JC need time to heave himself out of his chair. As soon as everyone sat down, he took charge again, asking the question that had been worrying Seth and probably everyone aboard.

"So when we return home we can assure ISLA that there is no need to quarantine us?"

"I expect so, Commodore, as long as we remain healthy for the duration of the voyage. ISLA may want to run some tests, of course, and confirm my findings. I shall initiate a course of antiviral treatment for all of us until we can be certain we have eliminated all traces of the prion."

Smiles broke out all over. They would not be pariahs, lepers, outcasts from their home world. That had been part of the problem — although far from all of it.

JC segued smoothly back into his speech, confident that it would be viewed by billions as soon as he returned to Earth. "Although mankind has been exploring the stars for more than a century..."

He lambasted Galactic by giving Prospector Meredith Tsukuba credit for making first contact with the centaurs and attributing sentience to them; he belabored the way she had then been abandoned to die and the way Commodore Duddridge had flouted ISLA rules by posting a yellow beacon, instead of a purple. He even lauded "young" Seth Broderick for his heroic rescue and the way he had clearly established that the centaurs were capable of speech, reasoning, and cooperation. He did not mention that he wanted to strangle the aforementioned young man for ruining the whole expedition and everyone aboard except Seth himself.

"I call on him now to make his report. Prospector Seth Broderick!"

Applause.

"Even before I went down to the planet's surface," Seth said, "Commodore Lecanard suggested that the Galactic expedition that preceded us had made a discovery that it did not wish to reveal — something extremely valuable. This was characteristically observant of him." *Soap him up before you push him off the plank.* "Commodore, sir, this gets us into legal matters. Is it possible to turn off Control's recording function for a few minutes?"

JC choked, coughed, turned scarlet, and finally managed to say, "Possible, yes. But it would be illegal."

Again Jordan interrupted, looking even angrier than before. "I was expressly assured that it was not possible. The ship's specs and ISLA's GenRegs say the same. This is your own doing? You were an IT engineer, once. You have been meddling with Control's software?"

JC put on an even harder internal struggle, but lost again, seemingly just before suffering an apoplectic fit. "I think there could be a way to suspend recording, but it has never been tested and I refuse to try it now. Let us have your report, Prospector!"

He had been given his chance.

Seth was not ready to report anything yet. "When you hired me, Commodore, you assured me that the crew, meaning the people present here, other than Meredith Tsukuba, would be sharing between them fifteen percent of the ownership of Mighty Mite Ltd. Is that true?"

"Certainly it is! Are you accusing me of being a liar?"

Certainly he was a liar, but men of his stature must not be accused without very good evidence.

"And will those shares make us rich?"

JC choked, gasped, spluttered… And whispered, "No."

"Why not?"

"Because there is nothing to share. Thanks to you and your hellish stupidity in proving that those freaks are sentient, ISLA will interdict the planet and there won't be any profits. You wanted to be famous. You wanted to go down as the first man in history to discover an intelligent species. Idiot! You really believe you're the first to find evidence of intelligent species in the galaxy? The trick is to back off quick and keep your mouth shut, but oh no, not you! Why do you think Indra keeps finding such wonderful stuff on Floren and yet never investigates the lesser continent? Why won't it even let its ships overfly it? Because they'd see fields down there, and roads, that's why!

"Why do you think Star Ventures never went back to Pixie, in spite of the terrific chemical feedstock they brought back on the first visit? Because they traded for some of them, and if the truth ever gets out, ISLA will fine them trillions, that's why.

"But thanks to you and your insanity, Mighty Mite will declare bankruptcy an hour after we establish radio contact. That goes for you too, boy! You may think you own the copyright on your plog, but the creditors will seize that as well, or tie it up in the courts for a hundred years. We're all flat broke together."

Seth ignored all the angry glares directed at him. "You too, sir?"

"Including me, yes."

What? For a moment Seth was stumped, and then he saw the way out. "But your wife is wealthy? Are your children?"

Still JC could not refuse to answer. "They have property, yes. What the hell have you done to me? I don't feel well…"

"I have done nothing to you, sir. We're discussing what you have done to us. Remember when we started, when we all dreamed of bringing back things of great value from Cacafuego, things big enough to make the expedition a roaring success. Were you planning to cheat us out of our cut?"

JC shrank back like a cowed dog. He swallowed a few times and nodded, growing older by the minute. He could not resist the truth compulsion. "Yes."

The audience sat up straighter on their chairs. Jordan opened her mouth but Seth raised a warning hand and plunged ahead.

"How? Cheat us how?"

"Greenhorn Corporation. It's a privately owned company that loaned Mighty Mite some of its start-up money. It has first call on any and all discoveries that we make. Mighty Mite is a worthless shell. Greenhorn would have taken all the profits and none of the debt. But that isn't going to happen, you idiot! If you'd left that woman to die and ignored the centaurs, Mighty Mite could have staked Cacafuego and then Greenhorn could have stripped it of everything it had. You had to go and play knight in shining armor. Now ISLA claims all samples, living or dead. We're still broke."

"True," Seth admitted. "Who owns Greenhorn?"

"Several people."

"How much do you control?"

JC looked around despairingly. "Twelve percent. It doesn't matter now."

Jordan said, "But it could have mattered very much. This was fraud you were planning! You were hoping to cheat us, and Mighty Mite's shareholders, and the banks and funds that had loaned it money?"

"A lawyer could call it that. My lawyers wouldn't. And I would have seen you each got a reasonable reward."

"You would have defined the 'reasonable' part of course."

Silence: Seth had made a statement, not asked a question.

Meredith chuckled, although she wasn't smiling. "I'm waiting to hear a motion that you be put outside to walk home, Mr. Lecanard."

"Control is still recording," JC said quickly. He, too, must smell the bloodlust in the air.

"So it is," Jordan said softly. "And since you have confessed to attempted fraud, you could now sell each of us two percent of this Greenhorn Corporation for the sum of one dollar and our promise not to sue. That is to say the six of us will pay you six dollars for your entire holdings. We could make that legally binding, couldn't we?"

Choke… Gasp… "Yes."

"Yes, let's do that," Hanna said. Her face was flushed as red as Betelgeuse and her fingers were hooked like claws. "Just on principle."

It took a little while to get the wording right, but Control pulled some precedents from its archives and approved the final brief text. Crushed, JC appended his sig, and so did the others.

"Commodore," Jordan said, "You are confined to quarters for reasons of health." Several people nodded, as if to confirm that strangulation was a definite health hazard. "You may go now."

Crushed, JC rose and crept out of the room. The captain moved to the head of the table.

"Control, I terminate this meeting and reverse its classification as the official wake. We will schedule a proper wake for tomorrow." She stared hard at Seth. "What have you seen that the rest of us haven't, Prospector?"

Seth grinned. No one else did, but he was feeling very good now.

"I've seen what Commodore Duddridge saw. As JC guessed, Duddridge had seen that Cacafuego did offer a hugely profitable discovery. You have just seen it start to pay off!

"Remember the first day we met, ma'am? We agreed that Ship's Rules should specify monkeys not monks, because people always play sex games. We also agreed that power games are popular too. Well, both sorts of games depend on telling lies. In the last few days, I have found myself in several very embarrassing conversations." He glanced around the table and saw that he had not been the only one.

"Eventually I realized that the mysterious infection was making it impossible for us to tell lies, even little everyday white lies. Duddridge talked with both Meredith and Mariko while they were infected. Meredith told me that he asked all sorts of personal questions." Seth glanced at her. "So you answered them, *and* you insulted him to his face, even though he held your life in his hands?"

"When I get my hands on him," she said, "Duddridge will be even dudder than he is now."

"He was supposed to be planning how to rescue her from certain death," Seth explained. "So what was he doing prying into her sex life? He had discovered that she could not refuse to reveal the most intimate details, as any normal person would, especially at a time like that. Of course, she had gone on record as saying that the centaurs were sentient, so he had an interest in making her sound irrational. But I think he had noticed what I noticed, that one of the signs of the prion infection was in an inability to lie. That would be disastrous for normal human relations."

"Yes, you would miss that," Jordan said drily.

"I have missed it," he admitted, "these last few days. I was frightened we had all suffered permanent brain damage. But yesterday I discovered I had recovered my lying skill as my health returned."

"That was when you told me Meredith wasn't much of a lay?"

"I hate you, Jordan Spears."

Jordan joined in the laughter. The mood of the meeting had made a dramatic about-turn. "Lying or not, keep talking."

"The real brainwave came when Reese told us about the prion. A prion really isn't living or dead, is it, Doctor?"

"No," Reese said. "It's an organic chemical. But it came from Cacafuego. ISLA will still claim it."

"No," Seth said. "You told us it is also terrestrial, a deviant form of one of our own brain proteins. Our brains did not originate on Cacafuego. You are one of the world's foremost biologists. By the time we return to Earth, you will have worked out how to mis-fold it to recreate the protein, and you will have pinned down the antidote you mentioned. You will patent both for Greenhorn. You say that you found no antibodies in our blood, so there can be no buildup of resistance. If you need to try it out to see if it works again, I'll volunteer for a second dose. Any discoveries you make regarding a human protein cannot be claimed by ISLA; they belong to Mighty Mite under the contract, and so to Greenhorn, and now we own a big chunk of Greenhorn."

Faces all around the table were bright with hope, yet shadowed by doubt.

Jordan put the conflict into words: "You're suggesting we profit by selling a biological weapon?"

"Oh no, ma'am. But think of all the police forces and security forces in the world. How much do you think they'll be willing to pay for a safe, reliable, and reversible truth drug?"

Reese answered. "Plenty." She eyed the captain. "But lovers might offer more."

"Let's stick to governments," Hanna said. "Letting lovers have it would be much too dangerous."

SPACE HEROES WED

June 4, 2378: An estimated viewing audience of three billion people watched the celebrated spacers of *Golden Hind* tie the knot today at the Illimani Paradiso in La Paz, Bolivia, one year to the day after their return from exoplanet Cacafuego. Former Captain Jordan Spears and Prospectors Seth Broderick and Meredith Tsukuba exchanged vows in a three-way civil ceremony attended in person by only a few close family members and former crewmates.

Invitations specified nineteenth century costume. Plog star Broderick was appropriately dressed as Victorian explorer Henry Morton Stanley, the man who rescued Dr Livingstone, and the brides wore crinolines of white starsilk, topped with diamond tiaras.

The happy trio later left for an undisclosed destination, rumored to be either Mr. Broderick's nuclear-powered yacht or his recently purchased castle in the Italian Alps.

Our titles are available at major book stores
and local independent resellers who support
Science Fiction and Fantasy readers like you.

EDGE Science Fiction
and Fantasy Publishing

www.edgewebsite.com

Our titles are available at major book stores and local independent resellers who support Science Fiction and Fantasy readers like you.

Alphanauts by J. Brian Clarke (tp) - ISBN: 978-1-894063-14-2
Apparition Trail, The by Lisa Smedman (tp) - ISBN: 978-1-894063-22-7
As Fate Decrees by Denysé Bridger (tp) - ISBN: 978-1-894063-41-8
Avim's Oath (Part Six of the Okal Rel Saga) by Lynda Williams (tp)
  - ISBN: 978-1-894063-35-7

Black Chalice, The by Marie Jakober (hb) - ISBN: 978-1-894063-00-7
Blue Apes by Phyllis Gotlieb (pb) - ISBN: 978-1-895836-13-4
Blue Apes by Phyllis Gotlieb (hb) - ISBN: 978-1-895836-14-1

Captives by Barbara Galler-Smith and Josh Langston (tp)
  - ISBN: 978-1-894063-53-1
Children of Atwar, The by Heather Spears (pb) - ISBN: 978-0-88878-335-6
Chilling Tales: Evil Did I Dwell; Lewd I Did Live edited by Michael Kelly (tp)
  - ISBN: 978-1-894063-52-4
Cinco de Mayo by Michael J. Martineck (pb) - ISBN: 978-1-894063-39-5
Cinkarion - The Heart of Fire (Part Two of The Chronicles of the Karionin)
  by J. A. Cullum - (tp) - ISBN: 978-1-894063-21-0
Circle Tide by Rebecca K. Rowe (tp) - ISBN: 978-1-894063-59-3
Clan of the Dung-Sniffers by Lee Danielle Hubbard (tp) - ISBN: 978-1-894063-05-0
Claus Effect, The by David Nickle & Karl Schroeder (pb) - ISBN: 978-1-895836-34-9
Claus Effect, The by David Nickle & Karl Schroeder (hb) - ISBN: 978-1-895836-35-6
Courtesan Prince, The (Part One of the Okal Rel Saga) by Lynda Williams (tp)
  - ISBN: 978-1-894063-28-9

Danse Macabre: Close Encounters With the Reaper edited by Nancy Kilpatrick (tp)
  - ISBN: 978-1-894063-96-8
Dark Earth Dreams by Candas Dorsey & Roger Deegan (comes with a CD)
  - ISBN: 978-1-895836-05-9
Darkness of the God (Children of the Panther Part Two)
  by Amber Hayward (tp) - ISBN: 978-1-894063-44-9
Demon Left Behind, The by Marie Jakober (tp) - ISBN: 978-1-894063-49-4
Distant Signals by Andrew Weiner (tp) - ISBN: 978-0-88878-284-7
Dreams of an Unseen Planet by Teresa Plowright (tp) - ISBN: 978-0-88878-282-3
Dreams of the Sea (Part 1 of Tyranaël) by Élisabeth Vonarburg (tp)
  - ISBN: 978-1-895836-96-7
Dreams of the Sea (Part 1 of Tyranaël) by Élisabeth Vonarburg (hb)
  - ISBN: 978-1-895836-98-1
Druids by Barbara Galler-Smith and Josh Langston (tp)
  - ISBN: 978-1-894063-29-6

Eclipse by K. A. Bedford (tp) - ISBN: 978-1-894063-30-2
Even The Stones by Marie Jakober (tp) - ISBN: 978-1-894063-18-0
Evolve: Vampire Stories of the New Undead edited by Nancy Kilpatrick (tp)
  - ISBN: 978-1-894063-33-3
Evolve Two: Vampire Stories of the Future Undead edited by Nancy Kilpatrick (tp)
  - ISBN: 978-1-894063-62-3

Far Arena (Part Five of the Okal Rel Saga) by Lynda Williams (tp)
    - ISBN: 978-1-894063-45-6
Fires of the Kindred by Robin Skelton (tp) - ISBN: 978-0-88878-271-7
Forbidden Cargo by Rebecca Rowe (tp) - ISBN: 978-1-894063-16-6

Game of Perfection, A (Part 2 of Tyranaël) by Élisabeth Vonarburg (tp)
    - ISBN: 978-1-894063-32-6
Gaslight Arcanum: Uncanny Tales of Sherlock Holmes
    edited by Jeff Campbell & Charles Prepolec (pb)
    - ISBN: 978-1-8964063-60-9
Gaslight Grimoire: Fantastic Tales of Sherlock Holmes
    edited by Jeff Campbell & Charles Prepolec (pb)
    - ISBN: 978-1-8964063-17-3
Gaslight Grotesque: Nightmare Tales of Sherlock Holmes
    edited by Jeff Campbell & Charles Prepolec (pb)
    - ISBN: 978-1-8964063-31-9
Gathering Storm (Part Eight of the Okal Rel Saga) by Lynda Williams (tp)
    - ISBN: 978-1-77053-020-1
Green Music by Ursula Pflug (tp) - ISBN: 978-1-895836-75-2
Green Music by Ursula Pflug (hb) - ISBN: 978-1-895836-77-6

Healer, The (Children of the Panther Part One) by Amber Hayward (tp)
    - ISBN: 978-1-895836-89-9
Healer, The (Children of the Panther Part One) by Amber Hayward (hb)
    - ISBN: 978-1-895836-91-2
Healer's Sword (Part Seven of the Okal Rel Saga) by Lynda Williams (tp)
    - ISBN: 978-1-894063-51-7

Hell Can Wait by Theodore Judson (tp) - ISBN: 978-1-978-1-894063-23-4
Hounds of Ash and other tales of Fool Wolf, The by Greg Keyes (pb)
    - ISBN: 978-1-894063-09-8
Hydrogen Steel by K. A. Bedford (tp) - ISBN: 978-1-894063-20-3

i-ROBOT Poetry by Jason Christie (tp) - ISBN: 978-1-894063-24-1
Immortal Quest by Alexandra MacKenzie (pb) - ISBN: 978-1-894063-46-3

Jackal Bird by Michael Barley (pb) - ISBN: 978-1-895836-07-3
Jackal Bird by Michael Barley (hb) - ISBN: 978-1-895836-11-0
JEMMA7729 by Phoebe Wray (tp) - ISBN: 978-1-894063-40-1

Keaen by Till Noever (tp) - ISBN: 978-1-894063-08-1
Keeper's Child by Leslie Davis (tp) - ISBN: 978-1-894063-01-2

Land/Space edited by Candas Jane Dorsey and Judy McCrosky (tp)
    - ISBN: 978-1-895836-90-5
Land/Space edited by Candas Jane Dorsey and Judy McCrosky (hb)
    - ISBN: 978-1-895836-92-9
Lyskarion: The Song of the Wind (Part One of The Chronicles of the Karionin)
    by J.A. Cullum (tp) - ISBN: 978-1-894063-02-9

Machine Sex and other stories by Candas Jane Dorsey (tp)
    - ISBN: 978-0-88878-278-6
Maërlande Chronicles, The by Élisabeth Vonarburg (pb)
    - ISBN: 978-0-88878-294-6

Moonfall by Heather Spears (pb) - ISBN: 978-0-88878-306-6

Of Wind and Sand by Sylvie Bérard (translated by Sheryl Curtis) (tp)
   - ISBN: 978-1-894063-19-7
On Spec: The First Five Years edited by On Spec (pb)
   - ISBN: 978-1-895836-08-0
On Spec: The First Five Years edited by On Spec (hb)
   - ISBN: 978-1-895836-12-7
Orbital Burn by K. A. Bedford (tp) - ISBN: 978-1-894063-10-4
Orbital Burn by K. A. Bedford (hb) - ISBN: 978-1-894063-12-8

Pallahaxi Tide by Michael Coney (pb) - ISBN: 978-0-88878-293-9
Passion Play by Sean Stewart (pb) - ISBN: 978-0-88878-314-1
Petrified World (Determine Your Destiny #1) by Piotr Brynczka (pb)
   - ISBN: 978-1-894063-11-1
Plague Saint by Rita Donovan, The (tp) - ISBN: 978-1-895836-28-8
Plague Saint by Rita Donovan, The (hb) - ISBN: 978-1-895836-29-5
Paradox Resolution by K. A. Bedford (tp) - ISBN:978-1-894063-88-3
Pock's World by Dave Duncan (tp) - ISBN: 978-1-894063-47-0
Pretenders (Part Three of the Okal Rel Saga) by Lynda Williams (tp)
   - ISBN: 978-1-894063-13-5

Reluctant Voyagers by Élisabeth Vonarburg (pb) - ISBN: 978-1-895836-09-7
Reluctant Voyagers by Élisabeth Vonarburg (hb) - ISBN: 978-1-895836-15-8
Resisting Adonis by Timothy J. Anderson (tp) - ISBN: 978-1-895836-84-4
Resisting Adonis by Timothy J. Anderson (hb) - ISBN: 978-1-895836-83-7
Rigor Amortis edited by Jaym Gates and Erika Holt (tp)
   - ISBN: 978-1-894063-63-0
Righteous Anger (Part Two of the Okal Rel Saga) by Lynda Williams (tp)
   - ISBN: 897-1-894063-38-8

Silent City, The by Élisabeth Vonarburg (tp) - ISBN: 978-1-894063-07-4
Slow Engines of Time, The by Élisabeth Vonarburg (tp)
   - ISBN: 978-1-895836-30-1
Slow Engines of Time, The by Élisabeth Vonarburg (hb)
   - ISBN: 978-1-895836-31-8
Stealing Magic by Tanya Huff (tp) - ISBN: 978-1-894063-34-0
Stolen Children (Children of the Panther Part Three)
   by Amber Hayward (tp) - ISBN: 978-1-894063-66-1
Strange Attractors by Tom Henighan (pb) - ISBN: 978-0-88878-312-7

Taming, The by Heather Spears (pb) - ISBN: 978-1-895836-23-3
Taming, The by Heather Spears (hb) - ISBN: 978-1-895836-24-0
Technicolor Ultra Mall by Ryan Oakley (tp) - ISBN: 978-1-894063-54-8
Ten Monkeys, Ten Minutes by Peter Watts (tp) - ISBN: 978-1-895836-74-5
Ten Monkeys, Ten Minutes by Peter Watts (hb) - ISBN: 978-1-895836-76-9
Tesseracts 1 edited by Judith Merril (pb) - ISBN: 978-0-88878-279-3
Tesseracts 2 edited by Phyllis Gotlieb & Douglas Barbour (pb)
   - ISBN: 978-0-88878-270-0
Tesseracts 3 edited by Candas Jane Dorsey & Gerry Truscott (pb)
   - ISBN: 978-0-88878-290-8
Tesseracts 4 edited by Lorna Toolis & Michael Skeet (pb)
   - ISBN: 978-0-88878-322-6
Tesseracts 5 edited by Robert Runté & Yves Maynard (pb)
   - ISBN: 978-1-895836-25-7

Tesseracts 5 edited by Robert Runté & Yves Maynard (hb)
- ISBN: 978-1-895836-26-4

Tesseracts 6 edited by Robert J. Sawyer & Carolyn Clink (pb)
- ISBN: 978-1-895836-32-5

Tesseracts 6 edited by Robert J. Sawyer & Carolyn Clink (hb)
- ISBN: 978-1-895836-33-2

Tesseracts 7 edited by Paula Johanson & Jean-Louis Trudel (tp)
- ISBN: 978-1-895836-58-5

Tesseracts 7 edited by Paula Johanson & Jean-Louis Trudel (hb)
- ISBN: 978-1-895836-59-2

Tesseracts 8 edited by John Clute & Candas Jane Dorsey (tp)
- ISBN: 978-1-895836-61-5

Tesseracts 8 edited by John Clute & Candas Jane Dorsey (hb)
- ISBN: 978-1-895836-62-2

Tesseracts Nine edited by Nalo Hopkinson and Geoff Ryman (tp)
- ISBN: 978-1-894063-26-5

Tesseracts Ten: A Celebration of New Canadian Specuative Fiction
edited by Robert Charles Wilson and Edo van Belkom (tp)
- ISBN: 978-1-894063-36-4

Tesseracts Eleven: Amazing Canadian Speulative Fiction
edited by Cory Doctorow and Holly Phillips (tp)
- ISBN: 978-1-894063-03-6

Tesseracts Twelve: New Novellas of Canadian Fantastic Fiction
edited by Claude Lalumière (tp)
- ISBN: 978-1-894063-15-9

Tesseracts Thirteen: Chilling Tales from the Great White North
edited by Nancy Kilpatrick and David Morrell (tp)
- ISBN: 978-1-894063-25-8

Tesseracts 14: Strange Canadian Stories
edited by John Robert Colombo and Brett Alexander Savory (tp)
- ISBN: 978-1-894063-37-1

Tesseracts Fifteen: A Case of Quite Curious Tales
edited by Julie Czerneda and Susan MacGregor (tp)
- ISBN: 978-1-894063-58-6

Tesseracts Sixteen: Parnassus Unbound edited by Mark Leslie (tp)
- ISBN: 978-1-894063-92-0

Tesseracts Q edited by Élisabeth Vonarburg and Jane Brierley (pb)
- ISBN: 978-1-895836-21-9

Tesseracts Q edited by Élisabeth Vonarburg and Jane Brierley (hb)
- ISBN: 978-1-895836-22-6

Those Who Fight Monsters: Tales of Occult Detectives
edited by Justin Gustainis (pb) - ISBN: 978-1-894063-48-7

Throne Price by Lynda Williams and Alison Sinclair (tp)
- ISBN: 978-1-894063-06-7

Time Machines Repaired Whie-U-Wait by K. A. Bedford (tp)
- ISBN: 978-1-894063-42-5

Vampyric Variations by Nancy Kilpatrick (tp)- ISBN: 978-1-894063-94-4

Wildcatter by Dave Duncan (tp) - ISBN: 978-1-894063-90-6